THE EDGE OF ME

OF ME

JANE BRITTAN

BLOWFISH BOOKS

BLOWFISH BOOKS

First published in Great Britain in 2015
by Blowfish Books
Blowfish Books Ltd, 15 Bennerley Road,
London SW11 6DR
www.blowfishbooks.com

ISBN: 978-0-9932334-0-1

Also available as an ebook
Mobi ISBN: 978-0-9932334-1-8
Epub ISBN: 978-0-9932334-2-5

A catalogue record for this book is available
from the British Library.

Typeset by Chandler Book Design

Printed and bound by Finidr, s.r.o. Czech Republic

For TB, Mouse, Roo and Stewie

To Delphine

Best wishes and Happy reading!

You think you can leave me, forget about me?
You are wrong. I will never let you forget.

Jane Britton

1

It's late but I'm still up.

I'm listening to them, listening to their voices rising and falling. I can hear them moving about the house, following each other, shouting.

My room's at the top of the stairs on the right, and if I leave my door open, I can hear them. There's a bolt on the outside but they don't use it any more. I know I should put my headphones on, read a book. But it's not that easy. Not when my name keeps coming up. And after my name, they'll go quiet for a bit and I imagine them standing down there, looking up at the ceiling listening for me.

I don't move a muscle. I'm a lizard on a rock.

In the morning, when I come down, it's quiet and Mum's sitting at the kitchen table in her coat, peeling an apple. A broken garden gnome lies on its side, watching her. She doesn't look up when I come in.

'Where's Dad?' I say.

She crunches into the apple and lets out a howl of pain. 'Bloody, bloody teeth. Mirror! Mirror! Quick!'

I unhook the mirror from the wall and she snatches it from me and examines her mouth. The rack of dentures that runs along the top has detached itself on one side and hangs there, half in half out, with apple peel sandwiched in between. She takes it out and I watch as she tweezers out the bits. She doesn't have any front teeth of her own and this happens a lot. But maybe not quite enough: like little shrimps in a rock pool, other pieces of food are hiding in there, a corner of toast, a curl of burnt bacon. Her face changes without teeth: dark pits under her cheek bones. She runs the dentures under the tap and makes me hold the mirror while she fits them back into place.

She smacks her jaws together to make good and a little web of spittle winds its way down her chin. She picks up the gnome.

Mum loves gnomes. She's filled the garden, front and back, with gnomes of every shape and size. This one is lying back rather provocatively, smoking a little pipe. She's squeezing the glue tube absent-mindedly when I say again, 'Where's Dad?'

'You're going to be late,' she says in Serbian now.

'Yeah, but where is he?' I say.

More to herself than to me, she mutters, 'Busy.'

On the table next to the gnome is a letter. The envelope's been shredded along the top. There are greasy kisses where the butter knife did its work. It has, I think, a French stamp on it and careful handwriting. There's no name, just our address.

I pick it up. 'What's in the letter?'

She grabs it, claws it up in her long fingers and pushes it into her pocket. 'Nothing.'

'Right,' I shrug. I butter a piece of bread and go back to my room to get ready. I sit on the bed and hear the familiar symphony of flushing toilet, zipping and buttoning of coats, all building to the kettle-drum finale moment when the front door is snapped shut. Silence.

Mum likes to keep the communication to a minimum, unless it's arguing with Dad. It's like she saves it up. But there never seems to be much left over for me. I mean, she *needs* me, they both do – my Serbian's not perfect, but it's a lot better than their English even after all this time and I translate for them when they need it, but otherwise they don't bother with me much. Most of the time I feel myself osmosing into the pattern on the curtains, leeching away into the carpet like a stain. Disappearing.

I think I get it now I'm older that what happens here isn't exactly normal. My family isn't like other families. In fact even the word *family* sounds a bit too cosy for what we've got going.

I know not everyone's *friends* with their parents. I'm sure loads of people have a worse time than I do.

But, you know.

I never cried when I was small, there was never any point in it. I couldn't reach her, I never could. You can't reach someone who doesn't want you to.

I guess part of it is that there isn't really anyone else. It's like we just got here, the three of us, and there was no one before us and no one around us. No history, no stories, no Uncle Engelbert or Nan or Auntie Minnie. I know. I've asked them. Over and over, in a kind of blank litany: about Serbia, their country, about the places they lived, what they did before I was born, before they came to England.

All they say, all they ever say is: 'It's past. It's gone. It's nothing.'

And I say then, 'So what about your parents?'

And they answer, 'Dead. All dead.'

'When? When did they die? How?' I say.

And they say: 'The war.'

The War: it's like a high wall that I can't see over. It's like the Great Wall of China and it runs all around us. And behind it, outside it, is everything I need to make sense of all this. It started in 1992 and went on until 1995. Like most wars, it was all about land and more land, and like most wars, hundreds of thousands of people were killed in it or lost their homes. I think my dad was a soldier then but he never talks about it.

I ask them why they came here and they look at each other and say, 'To start again.'

But starting again should mean something good, shouldn't it? Something brave and big but this isn't, and how do I know that? Because I know most other people don't act this way. Other people fill their homes with photos and relatives and Sunday lunches. They go places and they talk to each other and argue and make up again.

Not here.

At quarter past eight, I'm downstairs looking in the fridge for something to take for lunch when I see Dad in his pyjama bottoms in the garden; which is weird because he's never in the garden. But there he is making a fire in the bin and prodding at the contents with a sharp stick. The garden's small and paved, and in every crack in the stones, weeds of every sort rear skywards like they're trying to get away.

I open the door and he looks up.

'What are you doing?' I say.

He scratches at the scar on his neck and turns to face me. His eyes meet mine for a moment then flick away. They're watering from the smoke.

'Burning rubbish. Just rubbish,' is all he says and he looks down and coughs. On the ground is a pile of box files I've never seen before. He's pulling out papers, tearing them into strips and dropping them gingerly into the flames. Little scraps of black film fly up from the heat.

'I'm going now,' I say. 'Do you have any money? I need five pounds for a trip.'

Without taking his eyes off the fire, he takes out his wallet and offers me a note. And then, while it's still in his hand, he says, 'You OK? School OK?'

I stare at him. 'Um. Yeah. It's OK. Why?'

He sighs and then tries to turn it into a cough. 'You are a grown-up now.'

'What? What do you mean?'

'You will ... you will leave us soon I think. Leave home.'

'Well … I'm only sixteen. I mean – '

'When I was sixteen I was in the army.'

'But, but things are different here, now. I mean – '

'Maybe.' He shifts from one foot to the other. 'Maybe. Goodbye Sanda.'

Slowly I stow the money in the pocket of my jeans and go back into the house. I stop on the doorstep to tie my lace and behind me I can hear the crackle and hiss of the fire.

Lauren meets me on the corner.

She tugs at my sleeves and jumps up and down. 'I love that coat. Seriously! Where d'you get it?'

'Charity shop.'

'Cool.'

I smile, 'Maybe.'

'Really,' she says, 'looks great on you.'

'Thanks,' is all I can think of.

Unlike Mum, I *do* have all my own teeth. Apart from that, I guess the only really interesting thing about me – if you can call it that – is that I have odd eyes. I mean, odd like they're different colours: one green, one blue. It's funny but I think because of it, I can never quite get used to my face in the mirror.

Lauren's shorter than me and curvy. What's more she has a boyfriend: a real, bona fide, six-months-and-counting boyfriend. He *is* called Derek but you can't have everything in life. She has a laugh like bacon frying and five older brothers, all with red hair and freckles.

We met in the lunch queue in Year Seven. I was just

eleven and fresh out of primary school, and it all felt so big, so sussed. I wasn't ready for any of it. I wanted to be sitting on the carpet in a semi-circle with my thumb in my mouth listening to a fairy story. Anyway, there I was, staring down at the floor and shuffling forward with my tray, nibbling at my fingernails like some psychotic rabbit, and she started chatting to me in such an easy way that I felt myself loosen a bit. I said stuff back to her, even made her laugh once or twice.

That's what's so amazing about Lauren. If she wants to do something, she just does it. She doesn't stop to think about it or wonder whether it mightn't be better to wait until the rain stops or the next general election or whatever, she just does it. And more than that, she's the only friend I've got.

'What's now?' she says.

'Double English.'

'Wow. Double Joe. You going to talk to him today?'

I look sideways at her. 'What do *you* think?'

She pretends to consider the question. 'Umm, what *do* I think? Well. I would have to say … *no*. I would have to say that you will creep in early and sit at the back of the class and shove your head in *Romeo and Juliet* or whatever, until the lesson starts, by which time you'll know it's safe to look up and gaze adoringly at the back of his head, while dribbling onto the desk. Sound about right?'

I laugh and push her into a hedge.

'Listen lover,' she goes on, 'he's finished with whatshername. Everyone knows that. He's officially on the market, *and* if you don't get your act together soon, someone else will.'

Joe Mullins is gorgeous. Period. He started at our school a year ago and when I saw him it was like Christmas. I'd never been into boys before him. Not really. He has warm honey eyes and a surprised sort of smile. He's tall and dark and broad-shouldered and he has to be pretty much the boy every girl in our year wants to get with. And not only is he gorgeous but he is actually in a band.

This gives me – and – let's not kid ourselves here – practically every other sad sack in a mini-skirt and a pair of Ugg boots, the ideal and quite legitimate opportunity to ogle him from the safety of a crowd.

I think I've been in love with him ever since I saw him but as far as I'm concerned, people like me don't go out with people like him. It's like a dog with two heads. It's just wrong.

But there it is. He's in my head. Joe Mullins lives in my head, just behind my left ear.

It sounds stupid. I mean how can it be possible to feel so close to someone, like you know they're in the room before you see them, and to have hardly said a single word to them? But it's true, I do.

I turn to Lauren. 'Ah. So that's it? That's all he's waiting for? For *me* to ask *him* out? He's been waiting and hoping all this time? That's such a *joke*. He doesn't even know I exist.'

'Oooh! Jesus, Sanda. He's just a *person*. Just *talk* to him. You don't know – he might be a closet stamp collector or keep his scabs in a biscuit tin under the bed.'

'You mean you *don't*?'

'Just talk to him. It doesn't matter what about: coastal erosion, the Euro, anything. Just do it.'

I smile and shrug. We're getting close to the school gates and the familiar panic is setting in. Did I say I hated school? You see, not only can I not bring myself to actually communicate with the boy I have been in love with since Year Ten, but I'm pretty lousy at it generally. It's like someone dropped me off on the doorstep of Planet Earth without the Rule Book: the one that tells you how to get by in life and how to *communicate* with other people without getting a nosebleed or a hot flush. When Lauren spoke to me for the first time, it was the fourth of November. I'd been at school for two months and it was the first proper conversation I'd had.

She's poking me in the ribs now and saying, 'OK. Are you going to Rosie's party?'

'Er … no. Don't think so.'

'She says you can come if you want.' Tactful. Basically, what that means is that Lauren's got Rosie in a corner and talked her into saying that I can come if I absolutely have to.

'It's fine. I'm OK.' I go for what feels like the right mix of regret and indignation. But we both know I don't do parties. Ever. Because, in the unlikely event of someone actually inviting me, I'd find myself getting as far as the door, finger hovering over doorbell, and the mortifying, toe-curling embarrassment about what I was wearing, or what I would or wouldn't say, would send me running for the hills.

lekes out?

We go through the gates and Lauren's already waving to a couple of friends from her Art class. It's always about now I feel myself disappearing.

And yes, it is English first, and yes, I do get there super early and open my book. Not *Romeo and Juliet* but *The Wasteland* which seems highly appropriate considering my current social life. Miss O'Brien is standing at the front with the book as people scuff in and spill onto chairs and desks.

Joe comes in last and Miss wants to know why. I don't look at him but out of the corner of my eye I see heads go up, ponytails being fiddled with. He sits down in the front row and takes out his book. His neck dips, he pushes his hair back and his hands rest on his head for a moment. Square hands. I breathe out quietly. I'm alone in the room with him. Cat Power's playing 'The Greatest' and we're slow dancing and he's kissing me tenderly. I reach up and ...

'*Sanda?*'

'Um ... Sorry. I ... what was the ...?' Muffled laughter from the rest of the class.

'*Quiet!* What do you understand by a wasteland?'

Everyone turns to look at me. And I say without thinking, 'Er ... something neglected? Unattractive? Something nobody notices any more?'

For a split second I look at Joe. He returns my glance with a kind of puzzled smile.

The lesson pretty much curls up and dies for me after that. It lasts forever – it always does. When everyone's left, I pack up as usual and I'm weaving through empty desks, head down with bag and coat under my arms, when something completely unexpected happens.

'Hey.'

I look up.

It's Joe. Just Joe. All the air in the room gets hoovered out under the door. There's silence and somehow even the school noise stops and all the birds stop singing and hold their breath.

He's half playing with his phone but when I stop, he looks up and sort of squeezes himself in between the chairs and the front desk, and folds then unfolds his arms.

'Did you ...? Were you ...?' I say.

He smiles then and I manage to smile back but my face is burning. He crosses his arms again and backs into a little tray of pens which leap out onto the floor like angry salmon and scatter themselves under the tables. I'm down there before he is, pinching them up, and there's a red one that's rolled out of reach and I'm grabbing for it, and he's grabbing for it and then two things happen in quick succession. The first is that our hands brush and the touch of him, it's like hot tea on my skin and although he pulls away, I know the feeling will stay with me for the rest of the day; and the second thing is that Miss comes back into the room and sees us on the floor.

'What are you doing down there?' All I can see are her legs.

Joe gets up quickly and I follow, hitting my head on a table.

'Pens,' he says with a kind of yawning cough. 'We …
I dropped a load of pens.'

I slope up behind him and drop them into their box.

'Out,' she says.

I pick up my things and follow him out into the
corridor. 'Sorry,' I say.

'What for?' He's looking straight at me, smiling. His
dark hair falls forward onto his face. He's growing a
scrubby beard and it suits him. He looks way older than
sixteen. I lean against the wall and straighten myself up
to face him, then deciding this is too out there, I fall back
again into what I hope looks like a nonchalant pose. Then
my trainers go and make an ugly farty squeak on the lino.

I grin and snort a laugh. I'm an idiot.

'Just for … you know …'

He waits, shakes his head; looks up and down the
corridor. Message received: he wants to leave. I make it
easy. I say, 'Well … I'll … I've got …'

But he's not ready to let me go.

'*The Wasteland*. Crap isn't it?' he says.

Now I love poetry and I think TS Eliot is pretty cool
but of course I say, 'Huh! God Yeah! Shit.' Again I manage
a desperate piggy snigger.

He looks at me for a minute while I force myself to
face him with what I hope looks like a normal expression.

'Wow,' he says, 'I just noticed: your eyes.'

I look at him, waiting for an ironic laugh or a smirk.
Nothing. He looks back with an intensity that completely
takes me by surprise.

I struggle to fill the silence, 'Oh. Yes. I ... most people think they're odd.'

He smiles his surprised smile. 'No. No. They're good. Different. I mean different good ... you know ...'

Long pause while I try to look casual. I look at the notice board on the wall. Apparently the girls' toilets on the third floor block are out of use this week. Interesting. I see him shuffle a bit and I wait for him to leave but he doesn't.

Instead he says, 'Um ... Are you free Friday night?'

2

I need time. It's like I need a whole ten minutes before answering. I mean what does 'free' mean? Of course I'm free, I'm always free, but does he mean 'free' for him? To do something with him? *Together?*

I decide to play it cool. 'Friday night? Er ... yes ... I ... I think so. Um, is it your band?' Lifeline. Maybe it's just a gig – some hall to fill. I'd be making up the numbers.

He looks sideways at me frowning. 'No.'

'Are you ...?' I don't even know what I'm going to say next. And my teeth start chattering entirely of their own accord, beating out a tiny tattoo in my head.

'Are you OK?' he says.

'Mmm,' I squeak.

'So ...?'

I wrestle with my mouth and finally the words fall out of me like vomit and magically arrange themselves into a wormy little sentence.

'Yes, I'm free Friday.'

'Cool.'

'Shall I …? Do you want me to …?'

He looks at me, leans in, 'Sanda,' he breathes, 'what is it with you? I don't want you to *do* anything. I'm asking you out. Is that OK?'

I swallow air. My throat is dry.

'Where do you live?' he says.

'Um – 35 Durham Road,' I rattle.

'Can I take your number?'

The rest of the afternoon is a blur. I go to registration. I think I have a conversation with Mr Hall about Geography homework and sunspots but I can't be sure. *Real* Joe is filling my head, squeezing out *dream* Joe. But I'm not sure I want the real one. Not the one with the ex-girlfriend, who by the way, is French which makes her at least two hundred billion percent more interesting and sexy than anyone else on the planet. Not the Joe who, for all I know, may be a part of some mass class joke on me. I want the old Joe back, *my* Joe: the one where I'm in charge. I doze through French and leave school feeling sick with apprehension.

There's no wind and the sun hangs low in the sky as I walk home. The vomity feeling is replaced by something like a lorry-load of evil little midges wriggling and burrowing under my skin, biting and stinging me all over my body. I feel so hot that when I get in, I go to my room, take off my clothes and stand in front of the mirror in my underwear. I run my hands down my sides. No fleshy softness, no curves, nothing a boy like Joe would want to hold on to. What I see, what I feel, are bones that jut and scrape. Even in the laciest undies, even bending and arching my back and tossing my hair, I'd still look like a fourteen-year-old boy.

Anyway, all I own are jeans and T-shirts. Mostly from charity shops. I've been buying my own clothes forever. Mum doesn't do shopping – not for me. I certainly don't own anything that says *come get me tiger*, which is just as well really because Friday evening – if it happens at all – is probably going to be humiliating enough without me dressing up like some Beverley Hills hooker.

You see.

I've never kissed a boy.

I know what you have to do. I know all that. But the thought of it, of how to *be* with him makes my stomach turn.

All I want to do is hide. All I ever want to do is hide.

I do a lot of hiding; in fact I've made a bit of an art of it. I lie on the bed with the duvet pulled up over my head, my arms flat against my sides and my hands clenched into fists so tight that my knuckles crack and my fingernails cut into my flesh. I slow my breathing until the covers are barely moving and the space around my body is a warm orange bloom like a rind on cheese.

I *need* a rind, a shell, something to crawl into when the going gets tough. And yeah, I know I'm not Vin Diesel: I don't have to blow up a train or cross Niagara Falls in a waste-paper basket. I just have to *be with* people and talk to them. And what's so wrong with me that I can't even have a proper conversation with a boy I like? That I'm too congenitally fucked up to just say, *Yeah, I'd love to go out. Pick me up at eight?*

The thought of it shrinks me like a slug in salt.

I'm frying now and I shift and curl and push the covers onto the floor. I stand up and look at my reflection in the mirror again: drawn and rigid and scared.

And that's when I know I don't want to do this any more.

If it *is* real, if it's not a joke, then what am I doing?

Either I'm going to get an Xbox or take up online chess and effectively check out of the human race altogether, or maybe, just maybe, if I can actually stop feeling sorry for myself, then I can do this.

I practise my smile. I'm in the corridor, nonchalant, preoccupied, super-cool: 'Hey Joe.'

I say it a few times.

Fuck.

I think about texting Lauren but I'm not ready to have the conversation, not ready for her to get inside of it and tell me what she thinks.

I'm pulling on my clothes when I hear a scratching sound coming from the ceiling: like the sound of fifty pigeons on the march, then a thud and silence. I go out of my room onto the landing just as Dad's coming down from the loft, the ladder trembling under his weight. He's holding a great bundle of papers wrapped in a manila file and tied with string. He's still in his pyjamas, and the creases in his face bubble with sweat. I don't know what it is but there's something different about him. He seems distracted somehow – bothered.

He looks at the wall behind me, nods and hurries down to the hall where Mum's working the spray polish like a little Gatling gun. They snap and grunt at each other like a couple of seals then I hear the door to the sitting room bite.

Above me the black space in the ceiling yawns. I go to push the ladder back into place when I see something at the top. A wink of colour catches the ceiling light. A tooth of white in the dark hole: a photograph.

The ladder squeaks and crunches as I step up, the dry, sour smell from the loft coming at me. Blindly, I grope for the photo until I feel the cold silk of it on my fingers.

I snatch it down.

It's an old photograph. The colours were once garish but fading now: a blank orange background and a child, I think a girl, but I can't be sure. She can't be more than two or three. She's being held up to the camera. There are someone's thick fingers around her middle.

The picture isn't very clear because she's moving. Wriggling. Her face is a blur of white and I can't see whether she's laughing or crying. But her eyes – it's unmistakeable – they're two points of colour: one is green and one blue.

On the back of the photograph, a name is scribbled in loopy handwriting, a name I don't recognise: *Senka Hadžić,* and a date. And for a moment everything lags and stops.

A low wheezing tells me he's coming back up the stairs and before I can do anything, a hand comes around my shoulder and snatches at the photo.

But I hold on.

'What's this Dad? Who's this?'

There's a moment's pause and then he stretches his mouth into a kind of grin and points a grubby finger at the picture.

'You.' I stare down at it. After a moment he reaches and gently pulls at a corner. 'It's not important.'

He stuffs the picture into his back pocket, and I'm aware of my fingertips, hot and wet, where I was holding on to it. He's halfway down the stairs when I remember the name.

'But, Dad?' He turns on the stair. 'That's not my name on the back.'

The little collars of sweat are still there in the folds around his throat. There are the pale seams of the scar. He pulls out the picture, turns it over, studies it for a moment and then pads back up to where I stand and puts a hand on my shoulder.

'Senka Hadžić was your grandmother's name. She was taking the photograph. Back home.'

'So I've been there? Serbia? But you never told me …'

'Yes, yes, yes. Just for a little time. To see your grandmother. Just a short time.' He looks at me, his grey eyes wet and full. When he lifts his hand, I can still feel the weight of it like a bruise on my skin.

I make up my mind to get the picture back.

That night I dream about being held. I can't see who's holding me and I don't know why. It starts as an embrace: something benign and loving but then the grip around me tightens and binds and pinches until I can feel my lungs straining to breathe and my heart hammering in my chest. I wake up curled in my covers like some demented thing, and all around there's a dense blackness in my room, a breathing dark of familiar things made odd and strange: a table leg, the dressing gown hunched on its hook, and a thin whisker of light under the door. It's three o'clock in the morning.

I can hear noises: scraping, thudding, a sharp bark of wheel on wood, the press of stocking feet on the landing outside my room and the crunch of hinges on the ladder to the loft.

I lie there listening and under my skin, under the hum of blood, my bones freeze.

The next morning I sleep through my alarm and any careful thought that might have gone into choosing what to wear and how to wear it goes out the window because I'm late.

There's no sign of last night's activity, nothing to show that anything was moved or changed. Mum's at work and Dad's sleeping. I skip breakfast and head out the door.

Lauren's waiting: 'Oh my God what are you wearing? Did you get dressed in the dark?' she says, pulling my T-shirt out over my jeans. She fumbles in her bag, pulls out a lip gloss and offers it to me. 'Get some on Sand. You look like a bag lady.'

Meekly, I comply, and within seconds most of my hair is sticking to my mouth. She shakes her head, 'Did I hear you were seen talking to you-know-who yesterday?'

I nod, teeth grinding like wheels in my head.

'Well?' she says

'Well.'

'Well?'

'He asked me out.'

'*What?! No! Never!* Sand, that's great!'

'Er, no, basically it was a total disaster area. Total abortion. I just didn't get it …'

'What do you mean?'

'I thought he was asking me for help, you know… I just … Oh God.'

'*Help?*'

I nod and pick strands of hair off my lips and suck at the ends.

'But why would you think that?' she says.

I shake my head. 'I just couldn't – *can't* believe that someone like him might want to go out with me … d'you think it's a joke?'

She eyes me and I know the look: pity and exasperation.

'Why do you say that?' she says softly.

'Because in Joe-world I don't exist.'

'Oh my God.'

'What?' I say.

She's serious now. 'Look, this is going to sound really bad and you know you're my friend and all but the thing is you *won't exist* if you can't actually *say* things. Why can't you be like you are with me with other people?'

I just look at her and we walk on and suddenly the photograph of the little girl pops into my head and I feel that tightening around my chest.

'I'm going to try. I *am* going to try.'

'When are you going out?'

'Tomorrow night, Friday,' I say and my teeth start buzzing again. I bite down on my lip.

'Tomorrow?'

I look at her. 'Lauren, I can't believe he meant it. Why would he be into me? He went out with Camille for Christ's sake.'

'So?'

'She's so … so …' I want to say "French" but I end up saying miserably, 'Cool.'

'You're an idiot sometimes, Sand. *You're* cool too.'

We're at the gates now and there's that familiar smell of cheap deodorant, and the thronging of coats and bags.

'Cool? What are you *talking* about?'

She takes a breath and says, 'You've got potential, that's all. I mean I know *you* feel like you're on the outside but that doesn't always have to be like a bad thing. You're out there. You know, people do *see* you, *they* think you're cool, I don't know … independent. You just *have* to stop apologising.' She's going but then turns and shouts, 'Oh … and you're thin. You eat what you like and you're still thin.'

I stand there trying to take this in while Lauren's absorbed into the crowd. I'm heading off towards the music block for first period when I see him. He hasn't seen me. He's standing near Reception with his ex, Camille, and witchy tart Zoe Palmer.

He's laughing.

I stare at them and all my clever, quiet bedroom resolutions burst and dissolve.

I walk into the music block where Baroque orchestral music is on the agenda for this morning. From my place at the back, I can crane over heads and see them through the window.

When I get home, the house smells different. I walk into a sort of citrus fug that hangs over the hall. In the sitting room, Mum's standing by the window smoking. She's wearing a sheer black top with a high neck and she's scraped her hair back into a thick knot. My father's in his chair as usual but he's wearing clothes. He doesn't look up when I come in but keeps his eyes fixed on the floor. And opposite him, on the sofa, is another man. Which is weird in itself because apart from the guy who comes to read the meter, we never have visitors. He's wearing a dark suit buttoned across his chest, and when he moves the little buttons tug at their holes. He's almost as wide as the sofa but when he gets up, he's shorter than me. Under his suit, he wears a thin grey turtle neck sweater, so tight that you can see the hairs on his chest curled and flat like tiny springs. His cheekbones jut like shelves under careful blue eyes.

He waves a fat hand at me. Mum says, 'This is Andrija.'

'Er hi. Hi. I'm ...'

'Sanda. This is Sanda,' she says.

I give them all a cheesy smirk and begin to edge towards the door. Andrija settles himself back on the sofa and the buttons on his jacket squeak and pull at their threads.

Everybody looks at me.

Nobody says a word. Mum bends to flick her ash into a saucer and I see the outline of her backbone like tiny pebbles under her top.

As I back out of the room, I see her look at Andrija and he nods and says, '*Cytpa,*' which means 'tomorrow,' and then I hear Dad yell at her like I've never heard him before.

He's saying, 'No! You can't do this! You have to stop! It's enough! Just let it go! You knew this would happen one day.'

Then Mum's throaty bark cuts across him: 'You *listen* to me! You do what I tell you when I tell you! You will do exactly as you are told!'

Then come Dad's low growls and his mumbled responses. She always wins. I think it's because at the end of the day she doesn't care about anything *but* winning and how can you fight that?

But what are they on about, and *what's* going to happen tomorrow?

I run upstairs and slam the door. At first I fail to notice that my bedside table is missing and my chest of drawers has been emptied. My clothes are stacked in tidy bundles on the floor.

I go to the top of the stairs and call Mum but it's Dad who appears. His face is ridged and mottled. Behind him, I can see the dark bulk of Andrija standing in the room.

Dad comes up the stairs and suddenly he's standing too close to me, breathing hard. I hear a catch in his throat and he coughs it away.

'Dad, what's going on with my stuff?

'I am going to paint your bedroom.'

'Oh. OK. What colour?'

'Mmm?'

'What colour are you going to paint it?'

'White. White.'

I breathe. Something isn't right here. It's hurting my head.

'Who was that guy?'

He stares at me and blinks slowly. He looks tired. Exhausted. And I think then that like me, he's somehow flattened himself, hemmed himself into chair covers and lampshades.

'He is from Serbia. He worked with your mother a long time ago. He is helping us.'

'With what?'

'With …with immigration forms. There is problem with our …with our … status here. The police are making problems.'

'But I thought …?'

Suddenly he jerks forward and takes my hand in his and then just as suddenly lets it go.

I stare at him and he looks away. 'It's not a problem. Not a problem.'

But somehow I can't believe him. And very slowly I feel my breath starting to thin and my rib cage squeeze.

'What's happening tomorrow?'

'Eh?'

'What that man said … he said "tomorrow" like it was important.'

'That's when he's going to help us. Yes. Tomorrow.'

'So why were you and Mum arguing about it?'

He leans to one side and picks at a raised freckle of paint on the bathroom door.

'Sanda … I, we … I want to…'

'What? What is it?'

He sighs. I'm aware of Mum, now standing in the doorway of the front room below, clicking her tongue. Andrija is behind her.

'Nothing,' he says.

'Dad?' He turns. 'Can I have that picture? The photograph?'

'No.'

He goes back downstairs and closes the door.

3

I know life isn't always going to be this way. I mean practically everyone leaves school and grows up and passes their driving test and meets someone and has babies and a job and stuff. School is just school. It's just part of a long life and I bet when I'm forty-seven and I've got grey hair and bunions, I'll have forgotten all about it and the walk up the corridor into double English where I know he's sitting. But right here, right now, it's the hardest thing in the world, and if it weren't for Dad waking me at six o'clock in the morning to clear my room for painting, I don't think I'd have come in at all.

But here I am. And I'm supposed to be going out with Joe tonight and the only remotely comforting thing on the horizon, as far as I can see, is that it's half-term next week. So when the inevitable happens, when I learn it's all been some twisted joke and when the humiliation Geiger Counter racks up to eleven, at least I can go to ground for a week.

He's there and I walk past him to my table and because everyone's looking at me and I'm sure everyone's in on it, I don't look at him. But the air around him is buzzing, and I walk through it and I breathe him in, and a little Hope Fairy dances in front of me for a moment, then disappears in a puff of smoke.

I sit down in my place at the back.

Minutes pass. The smell of text books and floor polish.

He turns once to look at me, catches me looking at him, and a rosy flush spreads itself across my cheeks. I look down at once and scratch at a mole of gum on the desk with my nail. Zoe's answering a question in her fake husky rasp, David Moger, next to me, raises his hand and I get a choice whiff of sweat from his armpit.

I blank out.

The photograph I found comes into my head. Blurred and faded, washed out. It's funny – when I think about my childhood – about me in it – it's always like that: worn and bleached. It shifts and slips away from me when I try to reach it. A car journey; a doll with its hair cut off; picking blackberries on a railway line. The images are strung out in my brain like a bone necklace, joined by fraying threads. And the bones clatter and sing against each other but they never connect.

I'm breaking. Sometimes I think I'm breaking.

After a while, I'm aware of Miss O'Brien watching me.

'Are you with us, Sanda?'

I look up at that and so does everyone else. Zoe laughs, then everyone starts. Joe turns in his seat and I can't read him but at least he's not laughing. Not yet anyway.

Miss says, 'Get on with your work everybody.'

She comes over, puts a veiny hand on my paper, and I can see the rub of a wedding ring long gone on her left hand. She says gently, 'Are you all right, Sanda?'

I will myself not to, but as usual I don't do what I'm told, and my eyes start to prickle and fill.

'Um … I just … Can I …? Sorry.'

I push my table forward, haul myself out of my seat and leave the room and all the gushing and the gasping and the looks, and I walk. Long strides and I'm breathing hard and swallowing air. The corridor's empty and at every step I can hear the rise and fall of voices from the other sides of the doors.

The girls' toilets are on the floor above, and I'm at the stairs when I hear the sound of running behind me, and a voice: 'Hey! Sanda! Wait!'

I don't wait. I run up the stairs into the toilets, slam the door and head straight for the mirror. I turn on the tap, scoop a run of cold water into cupped hands and hold it against my face. And when I stop and look up at my reflection, Joe's standing right behind me.

'What are you doing in here?' I sniff.

He backs away to the door and stands against it.

'What is it?' he says, 'what's wrong? Is it me? If I'm anything to do with this … I'm …'

There's a clatter and a sudden push at the door from the other side and he braces his weight against it. 'Occupied! Sorry.' He turns back, swallows, says: 'I just wanted to …

you know – if it was me, something I've done …'

I turn around. 'I guess I thought … I don't know. When you asked me out, I just couldn't believe you really wanted … that it wasn't a joke … I know that sounds … anyway, thanks for …' I trail off.

'A *joke*? You thought I was joking? Why would I do that?'

I look at him. Water's dripping off my chin onto my collar. 'I don't know… I'm sorry.'

'Is that what you think of me?'

'No, God, no. I … I like you. I've always …' I stop myself, 'I was just so surprised you …'

A faint smile on his lips.

I think.

I fumble up my sleeve for a tissue and I smile back, 'Sorry.'

'Do you ever stop apologising?'

I shake my head. I'm aware that he's a little closer. His feet scrape on the damp floor.

My face is blotchy and my hair is wet. I push it back away from my face and I breathe. And I see him watching me. I know him watching me.

But there's that line again – that great big equator: clear as light and hard as coal and I don't know if I'm brave enough to cross it.

'So … you OK for tonight?' he says and I nod.

'Yeah,' I say. 'Yes. Please.'

'Cool. Seven OK?'

'Yes,' I breathe.

He smiles. 'I'll text you. See you later.'

I'm left staring at the Joe-shaped hole in the room as the door whispers to a close. I wipe my face for the last time and I go. I walk out of the door and along the corridor and down two flights of stairs and out through the entrance and into the open. Past the science blocks, up the steps and out onto the field. It's windy and the cold air storms into my lungs and stings my face. It wraps itself around me and carries me towards the edge of the field, to the shelter of a group of stunted trees, and leaves me sitting on the hard earth and wet grass where I can look back at the school. And I hold myself tight with my chin on my knees, and I don't think. I just sit there.

The bell goes. And a thousand bodies are on the move again.

I stay there tucked in tight for a long time. I stay there through one bell after another. I stay there as the rain starts out of low oyster clouds. I watch people moving across walkways and corridors in the distance: dark shapes like crows.

And when I'm soaked to my skin, I get up and I cross the field to the gates and out onto the street where sodden leaves line the gutters, and water pools in cracks in the pavements.

I know it. I have to cross that line.

There's still an hour of school to go when I reach home and push my key into the lock.

It doesn't turn.

I try again. And again. Whatever I do, I can't make it move. It's weird. It's like something's been shoved in the lock. I go out onto the street and look up at the house. I go back up to the door and try again. I ring the bell. Nothing. Mum's at work, but Dad should be home.

I bang on the door and shout through the letterbox: 'Dad!' He's probably sleeping in his chair. I try again, louder this time, 'Dad!'

Not a sound. And that would have woken him, should have woken him. I don't understand it. I mean he won't *be* anywhere. Apart from work, Dad never goes out. I move a grinning chimney-sweep gnome to get a look in at the front windows to see if I can see him in his chair. I peer through a little tear in the lacy nets and what I see there grips me with fear like I've never known. My throat closes and my body burns.

I smack my palms against the cold glass over and over until I can't feel them any more.

The room is empty.

Everything – papers, cards, trinkets, bits of broken china – all gone. All that's left is the sofa pushed against the wall. I look through to the kitchen and it's the same: pictures, pots, notes on the fridge about term dates, doctor's appointments, bank letters. One of the cupboard doors swings open on its hinge. The mantelpiece is bare, the floors are swept and all the surfaces are clean. It's as though no one has ever lived here. I don't know how long I stand there with my feet in the damp soil, beating a roll against the pane, listening to the sound ring out through empty rooms and bounce off bare walls.

4

My phone rings in my pocket. I pull it out and stare at the screen. It's Lauren. I can't pick up. I can't do it. Lauren's too real and this isn't real. It's utterly unreal. But the phone buzzing in my hand sort of brings me back to life, and when it stops ringing, I dial Mum. *'Unassigned Number'* comes up on the screen and there's a long beep. I try Dad's. The same. And again and again. I start to cry: panicky, choky gasps that fight for air.

I slide down against the wall of the house and put my head between my knees, trying to breathe. Someone shouts at a child across the street. The rain has stopped. A sweet wrapper drifts into view, works its way up the path, and the light catches it and shines gold in the cellophane. I reach for it and twist it into a knot. People pass, their footsteps slapping on the wet pavements, and the street is still again. I close my eyes and when I open them, I catch sight of something in the earth at my feet: something colourful dug into the dirt. A photograph –

or part of a photograph. I pick it up and brush it clean.

I see at once it's part of a picture of me.

I've never seen it before. I'm on the street outside the house, walking towards it. I'm wearing my old coat, carrying my bag, and I'm looking down, probably for my keys.

It's slightly out of focus and it's obviously been shot from above, from an upstairs window but without my knowing.

On the back, someone's scribbled a date. Two years ago last summer.

I have to get inside. I take a couple of deep breaths and get to my feet. A cramping pain like a stitch bites into my side, and I have to bend and breathe deeply waiting for it to go. Minutes pass and I hear the excited chatter of schoolchildren on the street going home, their voices floating through the air at me; a car pulls out from a space nearby.

When the pain's gone, I look around me for something to break the window. There's no other way to get in.

I pick up a stone, grip it in my hand and start hammering at the window. It's a lot more difficult than I thought it would be and after a few fruitless attempts, I lower my arm.

Something makes me look to my left across the fence. Our neighbour is coming up the path to her door.

'Hiya,' she calls, 'you all right? You locked out?'

'Um. um. Yes. Yes. I am locked out. Yeah.'

She blinks and looks me up and down. 'What time's your mum back? Do you want to come in and wait?'

Too much. Too many questions. I'm not in the right

mind to think up excuses and unless someone's going to do it for me, all I want is to be left alone.

'No. No thanks. It's OK thanks. I'm OK.'

She looks at the stone in my right hand and back at me. I drop the stone and it breaks in two. No wonder it didn't do any damage.

'Right. OK then. Well I'm in all evening if you need me. Just ring the top bell.'

I nod. 'OK. Thanks.'

She smiles at me in a half-hearted way and goes inside. Her door closes with a bang and I hear her opening the inner door and going upstairs.

I need help. I go out on to the street and look around. To my right across the road is a skip. It's full of timber, kitchen units and, on closer inspection, bits of plumbing tackle. With difficulty I pull out a tap and its pipes. I put it under my arm and I'm about to carry it back to the house when a woman from across the road comes out and stops me. I know her by sight but we've never spoken before. She's about Mum's age with dark circles under her eyes and she speaks with a northern accent.

'You moving?' she says.

'Um. No.'

'You're not moving?'

'Why do you ask?'

She shuffles around the skip, placing a proprietorial hand on the side. She's wearing slippers.

She looks at the tap in my hand. 'What are you doing with that?'

'It's … It's for a … um … '

'You should ask before taking stuff, you know.'

'Oh. OK. Sorry.' I go to return it but she pushes it back at me.

'I thought you were moving,' she says. 'Big van there this morning there was. Boxes coming out. You not moving then?'

'Er … no …well … maybe. Were my parents there?'

She looks at me in an odd way. 'They was in and out at first, then they went off in a fancy car with those blacked-out windows. Van finished up and went. That's why I thought you were off.'

'No.' Speaking is impossible when all I want to do is cry myself stupid. I feel my fingers tighten around the cold brass of the tap.

'OK, then,' she says, having obviously decided I'm not worth the effort. I nod and walk across the road to the safety of the hedge.

I bring the tap down on the window which cracks and breaks, scattering glass onto the sitting room floor. I reach in to open the window using the catches. They don't move. I try again and then remember they're locked. Crap. I hurriedly pick at the jagged edges and heave myself over the ledge. My palms are torn and bleeding, and when I get in, I have to spend a minute pinching out glass splinters and chips.

Once in the house, the strangeness overwhelms me. I almost collapse. I sit down on the steps into the kitchen and try to take stock. A van coming, my parents leaving in a fancy car: what's that all about? My dad's got an old Datsun he uses for his cab. That's it. They have no money, no savings. Mum works in a supermarket. What could they have been doing? Unless of course they've been *arrested*? For *what* though? I mean they never do *anything*, let alone anything that would be remotely criminal in nature. They go to work and they come home. End of. And anyway, what police cars have blacked-out windows? And a van? Boxes of stuff? All their belongings, anything that ties them to this house.

Except for me of course.

The house seems to press in on me. The emptiness is suffocating. In its stillness I hear echoes of Mum's voice shouting at Dad to pick up his coat, the rap of her heels, her fingernails tapping on the counter; Dad's low growl, the rattle of his cab keys on the stand in the hall; his heavy tread on the stairs when he comes home in the morning. And then what about me? What is there here about me? You could listen all day for it: only my quietness, my obedience. I think again about the photograph and I feel sick.

The house even smells different. The cloying mix of Dad's aftershave, glue and garlic are gone – and the place smells like old mushrooms. Mum's always been a hoarder – she keeps everything: bus tickets, old keys, labels, jam jars. But now there's nothing. It's as if all traces of the people who lived here this morning have been deliberately rubbed out. I force myself to go on into the back room: the same. Clean floors, blank surfaces, nothing in the drawers or cupboards but the odd pencil or crusted coin. The furniture they've left is stacked neatly to one side.

After standing in the middle of the front room for what feels like forever, I go upstairs. Apart from the bed now standing against the wall, my room is empty. He'd lied to me about the painting. Obvious now.

There are oily marks on the walls where posters and pictures have been. In places, there are little corners of glossy paper still sticking to the walls. All my things are gone – my books, my music, pictures, notes from Lauren. There are deep indents in the carpet where the bed and chest of drawers stood. A bluebottle slaps against the windowpane, trying to get out. I turn, and as I do, I notice something pinned up high on the back of the door: the photograph of the little girl, the hands around her waist.

I unpin it and put it in my back pocket. Then I take out my phone. I punch in 999 but something stops me from pressing Call. I remember what Dad had said when Andrija was here. No police. I can't do that to them.

There's something on the outside of the window: a black smudge. When I look more closely, I see it's a piece of charred paper. Down in the garden, there's the bin: a spire of dying smoke rising from it.

The back door is jammed in the same way as the front: a wedge of wood forced into the lock. I break the glass with a kick and climb through. The bin is full of blackened, burned paper: it's still warm but just cool enough to touch. I pull out a handful and it crumples to dust and disappears. A little way off, twitching in the wind, there's a thin crust of green card with my handwriting on it: part of my geography exercise book. I feel the bile rising in my throat.

I climb back in and go upstairs again.

On the landing, the picture of a small dog looking wistful hangs askew on the wall next to their bedroom. They must have forgotten to pack it. Or perhaps they don't want him either. Their room is the same: empty.

And then I see something: the loft ladder has been used again and not put back properly. I cross to it, reach up, drag it down and clamber up.

I switch on the light and pull the ladder up behind me. In the dim glow across the beams, there's a shipwreck of stuff: an old bed frame at the far end, a threadbare teddy bear grinning at me from a corner, a few pots and pans, a broken deckchair and half-empty cans of paint.

Things have been overturned; there are shiny scuffs on the boards where the dust has been disturbed. I follow the path towards some upturned boxes under the eaves at the back, and, kneeling on an old suitcase, I open up one of them. It looks like it's full of old tea towels. On one, Prince Charles's face beams up at me. The next box looks more interesting. For a start, written across it in capital letters, is the word: PRIVAT. It's lying on its side, but when I turn it towards me, I see that it's empty. A length of coarse string that bound it is loose on the floor. A few papers are scattered around.

This must be what he was doing the day I found the photograph.

My hands are still smarting from the broken glass, and one is bleeding again. When I lift out the Prince Charles tea towel to swab it, I notice something folded underneath: a yellowing cutting from a Serbian newspaper. I turn it over and on the back is a grainy photograph of a band of men in front of a truck. Some are standing, some kneeling on one knee – and in their hands are guns, large rifles. One man carries a scythe. They're wearing army- type camouflage jackets, some wear berets, some balaclavas, their faces hidden. They look proud, resolute: like they belong to each other.

In the front row in the middle, looking straight at the camera from under heavy brows, I see my father as a young man. He looks kind of fierce: like someone you wouldn't want to mess with, like he can't take a joke.

The picture makes my flesh crawl. For a while I'm distracted from everything else while I peer at it.

Underneath, there's a list of names corresponding to the men but the name under my father's picture isn't his.

Along with the names, is the word Škorpioni – Scorpions. I lift the cutting out carefully and put it to one side. Beneath it are a few other papers, bills, some old pamphlets in Serbian but nothing else that feels important.

I pick up the cutting, fold it and tuck it into the pocket of my jeans along with the photo.

Silence.

Then a car horn blasts on the road below and a man's voice shouts a rebuke. Something about the ordinariness of it makes me want to cry again.

And as I squat in the dim light, there's a sound from downstairs. A scraping, then a couple of thuds, something splintering. Then footsteps. Voices. Men.

5

My first thought is that it's the police come to look for me, to take me to my parents where this whole thing will be explained. I get to my feet knocking the bulb which swings angrily from side to side, then goes out, leaving me in darkness.

They're coming upstairs now. They aren't police. They're speaking Serbian.

I shift back on to my knees as quietly as I can and I wait.

I couldn't close the hatch behind me as it was too stiff. I have to hope they won't notice. They're directly below me now, and through the crack I can see one of the men quite clearly. I recognise him at once: short and broad with huge forearms: it's Andrija from the other night. Andrija, who talked about *tomorrow.* Is this what he meant?

He seems agitated. Uptight. He keeps patting at his face and neck like he's putting on aftershave. It's funny but without knowing why, I know I should fear this man. I remember the way he stood in the doorway with Mum as I spoke to my father. He's used to having people afraid of him.

I can only see the back of the man he's talking to. They're speaking in low voices and I can't catch what they're saying. The other is taller, with a shaven head and a tattoo of what looks like a crab on the back of his neck. They go quiet for a moment, then I hear them tramping downstairs. There is the sound of doors banging, then nothing.

A sudden buzzing in my pocket makes me jump. I pull out my phone and see it's a text from Lauren. A little bleep from across the ocean in the world of Normal, but I'm way too upset to cross over from where I am right now. I shut it without looking at the words and I'm just thinking what to do when it rings in my hand.

Without checking the caller, I answer it in a whisper, 'Mum?'

'Er ... No ... it's Joe. Are you OK?'

'Joe. Oh Joe. Yeah ...Um ...Yeah. How are you?'

'It's just, I texted you? After ... Did you get it?'

'Er ... er ... No. I ...'

'Oh right. OK.'

He sounds annoyed. Disappointed?

'Joe, no. It's not that ... I haven't ... I ... it's just something's happened and I just don't know what to ... I mean, I got home from school and I ...'

That's it. Right there. I can't say any more just then.

'Sanda?'

It's nice to hear him say my name. Kind of comforting. I force myself to speak and, in fits and starts, I tell him what's happened.

'Jesus! Where are you now?' he says.

'I'm hiding in the loft.'

'I'm calling the police.'

Dad's in my head now. 'No! No police. I don't … I just don't want to …'

There's a pause and I can almost hear him thinking then he says, 'Don't move. I'm coming over.'

'No … I … um … I'm sure it'll all be fine. Don't worry. I don't want …'

I try to sound like I'm on top of it but I don't think it's fooling him.

'Shut up Sanda. I'll be there in ten.'

He hangs up. Almost immediately my phone goes again and it's the text from Joe – sent at four o'clock.

Hi – It's Joe. Looked for you after school. See you later x

It's beyond mad, but I'm suddenly gripped with a pressing need to look at myself in a mirror.

Gingerly, I push the loft ladder down and descend. The house is quiet. A quick peep in the bathroom mirror confirms my suspicions. I *do* look dreadful. My hair is a mess and my face is streaked with black from my eye liner. I smooth down my fringe and wipe my face. Just then, I think I hear something downstairs.

I go down into the hall and see where the front door has been shouldered open and wedged back into place. Little spines of split wood poke at angles from the frame and decorate the floor under my feet.

The emptiness hits me again. It's so alien, so completely altered that I can't even see the room it used to be. It's gone: that shell, that rind that I could crawl into, and all that's left is me, standing in some vacant room, and everything that ever made sense is gone.

That's when I realise they're still in the house. A noise from the kitchen makes me jump and I make for the broken door. Andrija's too quick for me. He pins me in a powerful hug and the strength of him winds me. I curl over like a prawn, my skin tight over my bones.

He wheezes into my ear the words in English: 'Steady, steady Sanda. No need to worry. I not going to hurt you.'

He smells of garlic and it's making me gag.

'Let me go!'

He loosens his grip a little and propels me into the front room, claps me on both shoulders and steps away. The other man hovers by the door. I'm breathing hard and a kind of sick dread is pushing its way through my body and pricking at the ends of my fingers. My mouth is dust dry.

'Who are you? What's going on?'

He considers me calmly for a minute, patting at his face so his jowls shudder.

'You know me? I was here … and this is Boris. Your parents have gone away. No problem. No problem. I'm come for you.'

I stare at him, 'Sorry? What? I don't understand …?'

Boris picks his nose and watches us impassively.

Andrija goes on: 'Is simple. They have to go away, don't want to be found right now. I help them. I help you.'

He opens his mouth to smile. I can see a mesh of fillings in his teeth.

'Where are they? Dad said you were helping them with their papers, something to do with immigration?'

There's a pause. His blue eyes are on me. Boris coughs, spits on the floor and the little gob of phlegm catches the light.

'Where are they?' I say again.

'Mmm?' He seems distracted. Boris brings over a small rucksack and pitches it at Andrija's feet. Andrija squats down to open the bag. 'Home. They've gone home.'

'To Serbia?'

He looks up, nods and pushes himself up. In his hand is a half-empty bottle of Coke. 'Have a drink. You coming for a ride.'

'I don't want a ...'

They're slow but they're quick and as I go to run past them, Andrija pulls my hair and I'm jerked back against the wall.

'Yes, yes. Everyone disappearing. Like magic show. Come on Sanda. Open your mouth. Open it.'

'I don't want to drink it!' I'm shouting now.

He motions to Boris to hold me and he takes my jaw in one hand and squeezes until I have no choice but to open my mouth. I spit and gag and bite but a fat finger pushes on my tongue and the liquid is poured into me. My body stiffens and I retch but it reaches my stomach all the same. Cold and sharp. He doesn't stop until I've choked down the lot and I'm reeling. He loosens his grip and I find I can't stand up straight. I start to keel over. Andrija pulls down the upturned sofa and shoves me onto it. He pats me on the head: 'That's it. Good, good. Will help you sleep.'

Pins and needles in my legs. My palms tingle and my stomach gurgles and bloats. My head's fuzzy like I'm under the water in the bath. The walls are water and the floor is water and it's lapping at me, pulling me, swallowing me.

I dream about Joe. We're in a Western film, being chased on horseback, high in the Rocky Mountains. But I'm not on a horse at all. I'm on one of those rides they have outside the supermarket: a jeep thing. All it can do is buck to and fro, and in the meantime, Joe is riding off into the distance and I have to watch him go. I'm going to be caught. The bad guys are closing in on me. I see their hands tight on the cracked leather reins, their smiles: stale food between their teeth. Joe is far away in the mountains now. I'm calling for him but no sound comes out. I'm kicking out in frustration but the car is still bouncing back and forth.

I wake up and the bouncing doesn't stop, and I realise I'm sitting up wrapped in a blanket with my back bumping against a ridged metal surface. We're moving.

It's dark but every so often light flashes upwards through torn seams along the walls. Headlights, I figure. I seem to be in the back of a large box van tightly packed with stuff: odd bulky shapes turret around me. Right next to me is a large, long sort of cupboard. Every so often, it knocks against me as we turn a corner.

I can just hear the faint sounds of a radio: 'Islands in the Stream' – one of Dad's favourites. As I come to properly, I become aware of three things in rapid succession: one, that I need the loo; two, that my throat is achingly dry; and three, that a dim bundle in a blanket, across from me, wedged in between the furniture, and what looks like one of those life-sized china dogs, is another person. I can't see the face because the light is so bad and the body is curled away from me with its legs drawn up to its chest.

Just then we brake sharply and I hear raised voices from the cab in front. The sudden stop makes the china dog lurch forwards onto the body in the blanket which moves drowsily trying to shrug it off. As it does so, I see a mass of dark hair.

Joe.

6

'Joe? Is that you?'

He turns to look at me, rubs his face with both hands. 'You're awake at last,' he says. In the momentary gleam of the headlights I see him clearly. His hair is stuck to his forehead. He shifts back and sits up. 'Sanda, *what the fuck*?'

The dark presses in on us. I swallow and say, 'What are you *doing* here?'

'What am *I* doing here? What are *you* doing here?' He hangs his head and laughs weakly. He looks back up at me. 'I mean, we do English together, you *seem* normal enough. I … I ask you out, I call you and you're trapped in your attic, and the next thing I see is you being carried out of your house by two guys and thrown in the back of a van. So, er … you first, what's going on?'

'I don't know.'

'OK.'

'How did you get in here?' I say.

'Well. They slung you in. I waited till they went back

in the house and I just jumped in. I couldn't think what else to do. Stupid, really fucking insane thing to do, but … I don't know. Then I couldn't wake you. I untied you but …' he trails off. 'I've been waiting for you to wake up.'

There's a silence and I know he's waiting for me to say something but my brain and voice just won't catch up with the shock of the past hours.

After a while, I cough and say quietly, 'I think they're taking me back.'

'Back?'

'That guy. I know him. I mean I met him. At home. I think he helped my parents to −'

'Back where?'

I croak, 'Serbia. I think. Serbia.'

He slams back against the metal ribs on the van wall and the sound echoes around us.

'I'm sorry,' I say because that's what I always say. I always have a 'sorry' ready, just inside my mouth like a wad of gum, and all I have to do is reach in and pull it out.

'You're sorry? OK. Why? Why are *you* sorry?'

'Sorry. I mean … I'm sorry you got mixed up in …'

'Right.'

We sit unspeaking for what feels like a long time. The total mortification of it all makes me dig my fingernails hard into my palms. It's eating me alive. It's actually feasting on my internal organs − ripping them out of my body and chowing down on them with gusto.

Eventually he says, 'So *why*?'

I leap on it. 'Why?'

'Yeah, why? I mean, what's happened? Your house –
why was it empty? Why did they go? Why did they …?'

'Leave me? I don't know. My dad said there was some
problem with their … status … immigration … But I
really don't know.'

'What, like the Home Office?'

'Maybe.'

'But don't they just send you a letter? Or … make an
appointment … it's not the Mafia for Christ's sake.'

'Joe. I don't know.'

He must hear the crack in my voice because he slows
down a bit, says, 'Well. Yeah. Yeah. I'm sure it'll be fine.'

'Yes.'

He says nothing more for a while although I can hear
him shuffling and fidgeting. Then he looks at me and I know
exactly what he's going to say because it's hanging in the
air between us like a big neon sign. 'Listen, Sanda. Is there
something you're not telling me? I mean, are they – were
they – in some sort of trouble? Your parents, like bad stuff?'

I take a breath. 'That's the thing. They're so ordinary.
They're so … dull. They don't *do* anything. Mum works
– worked in a supermarket – and Dad drove a cab. I can't
believe they were *involved* in anything.'

'And they didn't leave anything? Like a letter?'

'Nothing.' I'm not ready to talk about the little girl
in the photo.

'Nothing,' he echoes. The silence between us just gapes.
Until he lets out a sigh, says again, 'It'll be OK, Sanda.
I'm sure.'

'Thanks.'

'They'll have to let you go. They'll never get you out of the country.'

'Maybe,' I say. And I think again about that line separating us, and wonder if maybe it's not between us but between me and the rest of the human race.

I start to cry quietly.

Joe crawls towards me in my corner and pats me awkwardly on the shoulder. 'Sanda, it's OK. It'll be OK.'

I peer back at him in the gloom. He stands up, steadying himself on the furniture around us. 'Don't suppose you've got your phone?' he asks.

'No. You?'

'Dead. You were my last.'

I stand up. We're moving fast now and I have to grab him to stop myself falling over.

'Are you OK?' I say.

'Shut up Sanda.'

He wraps me up and holds me, my face against his chest, and then, very slowly, awkwardly, I inch my arms around his back, my hands stiff and tight. I breathe him in: leather and soap. I grow on him like moss on a stone.

I can hear the radio in the cab up front, tinny and persistent. Reluctantly, I pull away and sit back down against the side of the van.

'They'll have to stop soon,' he says. He presses his watch and his face is illuminated in its blue flare. 'It's seven now, and I was at your house about quarter to five, so they probably know whatever they gave you will have worn off and they'll want to come and check.'

'So, when they stop, what then?'

'I don't know,' he says. 'I'm not fucking James Bond.'

'Right. No. Sorry.'

'Stop saying sorry for Christ's sake.'

'Sorry.' I twist my hair round my fingers till it hurts. Then I say, 'Joe, I know you don't have the answer. I know you're not fucking James Bond.'

He laughs. 'He's not my type. Look, here's what we do: we make a racket in the back here. They stop. They open up and we run for it.'

'OK,' I look around. 'How about him?' I point to the china dog.

'Genius.' He picks up the dog, lifts it over his head, mouths, 'Ready?' at me, and throws it against the side of the van. Nothing happens for a moment, then we feel the van slow down and stop with a jolt.

We stand on either side of the doors, our backs against the van walls and wait. My chest hurts and I'm fighting not to close my eyes.

The doors are flung open. I smell diesel oil, strong cigarettes like the type Dad smokes, and salt night air. A torch beam rakes the darkness.

'Hey?'

Everything happens very quickly after that. Andrija climbs in, his face in shadow. Joe lunges towards him, smacks him in the jaw, and he reels backwards and falls.

I'm paralysed. I can hear Boris calling from the cab.

Joe reaches across for me. 'Come on Sanda!'

I jump down, stumble, pick myself up. Andrija's back on his feet. He takes a heavy swipe at me but misses, and I start sprinting after Joe into the night along a motorway verge with the taillights of cars whisking past. After a few minutes, he hauls me away from the road and up. We charge over a low fence and start scrambling up a steep bank. The night is clear and the sky is full of stars and I go up that slope like a mountain goat, my heart pounding, and I can hear the blood singing in my head as I climb.

Below us, on the motorway, there's the low drone of traffic grinding the tarmac. And above us, beyond the ridge, fields, and sheep like little matchboxes. I push myself up on sods of wet earth, all the time watching Joe's heels just ahead of me.

I can hear Andrija and Boris behind us and I make the stupid mistake of looking back to see how close they are. If I hadn't done that, then everything might have been different but I do, and as I do, I lose my footing. I hit my head on something metal and sharp jutting out of the ground, and I close my eyes against the pain. I try to get up but the ground is holding on to me. Joe's yelling my name but I just want to sleep. I'm drifting. I'm being dragged along the ground then lifted up.

Oblivion.

Rolling. Ground shifting under me. Swaying. I lean forward as much as I'm able and throw up. My head feels hot and tight like I'm wearing a close-fitting hat. It's lighter here. There's blood on my T-shirt. I remember banging my head. We're moving but not moving and as I try to edge away from the reek of my own vomit, I hear a shrieking caw in the distance: a seagull. Seagulls. I'm back in the van but I think we're on a boat.

I struggle to sit upright. My hands are tied to the bars on the sides. They've used plastic straps like you get on boxes – impossible to get loose without scissors and another person to do the cutting.

I call softly, 'Joe? *Joe?*'

No answer. Just the urgent screaming of the gulls from way overhead. Louder this time: 'Joe!'

Nothing. I lean back and close my eyes. *Stay calm. You're OK.* My head's throbbing and my throat's dry, and I can feel tears of panic coming. I try to put together what happened: we got out of the van. We were being chased up the slope in the dark. I remember falling, hitting my head, Joe calling to me, and then nothing. He was ahead of me. He must have got away. And there in the back of a dirty removal van with blood on my face and sick in my hair, I sob out everything. The aloneness mostly – that aloneness I've always tried to convince myself was cool, was how I liked it: it meant I didn't need anyone. I'd watch the way Lauren's family were, hugging each other all the time, laughing and stuff, and I'd say: '*It's not for me – I'm not that insecure …*' Insecure? I wrote the fucking book. I've got nothing and no one, and even Joe who made it better for a while is gone.

I take a few deep breaths, swallow tears. I *am* in this on my own. So what's new? I've always been on my own.

I'm going to have to rely on myself to get out of it.

But the thought that I've been trying to bury since this all started comes bouncing right up: *get out and go where, Sanda? Escape to what?*

That makes me think about the cutting of Dad in my pocket: the group of men with their guns and camouflage, the different name. Dad in his pyjamas at three in the afternoon watching some crappy soap on the telly; Dad always rubbing at that scar on his neck; saying good night without looking at me. He never really looked at me. He always looked past me. What happened to make him that way?

It must have been something bad – someone or something that made him close up like that. Unless. Unless he's the bad one? All that endless fighting with Mum, those anxious, whispered conversations in the kitchen. Which of them wanted to leave without me?

What were they mixed up in? And if they're not who they say they are, then who am I? What kind of parents would just abandon their child? Like I'm nothing to them?

Maybe that's exactly what I am. Maybe I'm not their child at all.

And then the next question is so obvious, I don't want to ask it. I'm not going to ask it. Way in the back of my mind, I pull open a heavy wooden drawer, file it away for a later date, and slam it shut.

There's a shout from outside.

A man's voice calls, 'Oi! Off the car deck please sir!'

Andrija's voice in English – trying to be nice: 'I'm sorry. I forgot my wallet. I'll be quick.'

He's opening the doors.

I call out, 'Hey! Help me! HELP ME!'

In a second, he's inside standing over me with balled fists. He says in Serbian: 'Hey. Listen to me. You listening?'

I say nothing.

'Let me explain to you,' he hisses. 'It's easy. Why are you making it difficult? All you have to do is keep still and shut up.'

The sting of salt on my cheeks. His breath filling up the space between us. He brings a handkerchief from his pocket and crouches down. I think he's going to wipe my face but instead he pushes the cloth over my nose and mouth and holds it there. There's something on the cloth, something sweet-smelling but overpowering. And this time I don't fight it. I breathe it. I pull whatever it is into myself, under my skin, and it burns and snatches at my throat and my chest but in the end there's nothingness and that's just the way I want it. I want to go to sleep. I don't ever want to wake up.

The last thing I see is Andrija's face and it merges in my head with my father's and with the picture in the cutting.

7

Someone's shaking me awake. The van's not moving.

'Sanda?'

'Joe?'

I open my eyes. The light's dim and I feel him before I see him. He's got scissors and he's bending over to untie me. And I feel his hand. Soft and rough, it folds mine inside it.

'I thought you'd got away,' I say, 'I thought you'd ...'

'No. They ... they got me. I wouldn't have gone without ...'

'But where were you? I called you.'

He hesitates. He looks really shaken. There's sweat on his neck. He sees me looking and rubs his throat.

'They ... they beat me up. I've been on the floor in the cab under the seats with a gun to my head most of the time.'

'Oh my God, Joe.'

There's another wait and it's like he's thinking about

telling me something but then he stops himself and says simply, 'Don't want to talk about it. OK?'

'OK.'

'They let me up on the boat to … to wash and stuff. They said if I made a move, they'd kill you.'

'Oh Joe. I'm sorry.'

I feel his hand tighten around mine. 'Are you OK?' he says. I get a sense he's recoiling ever so slightly. I guess I smell pretty bad.

'Um, yeah. I think so. I may need a bath in the near future.'

'You never looked better.' It's good to see him smile. 'Listen, they've stopped at a service station. We're in Belgium I think. I don't know where we're going. They won't tell me, but they've said you can get washed and get some clothes and food and stuff. They've got showers here. Can you walk?'

He helps me to my feet, grabs a blanket from a pile on a cupboard and wraps it around me. He gives me a plastic carrier bag. 'They got you some clothes and a towel.'

'OK.'

He helps me down from the van and I make my way across the short stretch of concrete towards the welcoming entrance to the service station.

'Where are they?' I say.

'Watching.' He leads me to the showers and gives me a few coins. 'Another thing …'

'What?'

'Do you … do you know someone called *Branko*?'

'No. Why?'

'Nor me. But they think I'm working for him.'

'I've never heard the name before. Maybe it isn't a name. Maybe it's a company or something?'

'Maybe. I don't know.' He gestures to the showers. 'I'll let you go. Knock yourself out.' He laughs weakly and stands back.

The tiles are cracked and greasy and the plughole is full of hairs but at least I'm a bolted door away from them. I look at myself in the mirror and take stock. Blood, tears, vomit. My left eye is swollen, and the cut from my fall shows purple and blue. I'm a mess. Carefully I pull out the newspaper cutting and the photograph from my pocket. I throw away my old clothes, but somehow it's really important that I keep these pictures. They're a kind of talisman, connecting me to something. A kind of answer – although what the question is I have no idea.

The hot water feels good and I emerge from the shower block in my new clothes, the cutting and the picture now safe in the pocket of a candy pink track suit that's far too small for me. Joe's face tells me all I need to know about how I look. Boris is with him and hustles us towards the van where Andrija is waiting.

He looks at me approvingly. 'Good, good.'

I say in Serbian, 'Andrija. Please?'

He looks at me with his head tilted sideways like a fat bird, 'Hmm?'

'Please, let my friend go. You don't need him any more. Take me to my parents. He can go.'

Joe, who's looking from Andrija to me, says, 'Sanda, I know what you're on about and no, I'm not leaving you. Not until you're with your folks,' and to Andrija, 'I'm not leaving her.'

Andrija shakes his head and says to me in Serbian, 'You think *you* can decide what happens? Your type doesn't give orders to me.'

'*What?*' I say.

He thrusts his face in mine and I can see close up his furred teeth, pitted flesh, and smell the sweat on him.

'You'll know soon enough what you are. And this man,' he looks at Joe, says in English, 'I know who this man is. I know who's paying you.'

Joe raises his hands in exasperation and says, 'I don't know what you're on about.'

'Mmm,' Andrija grins, and turns back to me. I try to step away but his hand is clamped on my shoulder. He whispers in English, 'Why you think your parents left you?'

A great pit opens up and I'm on the edge looking down into a black nothing.

'I … I …'

'Mmm? Why do parent leave child?' He tightens his grip on me and I feel his fingernails burrow into my skin. He leans forward, lowers his voice and it's poison: 'Because they don't want you.'

I can feel Joe's sympathy or something like it and I don't want it. I want to fall into that pit and have the earth close up over me. Andrija shoves me against the side of the van and hisses in my ear: 'You want to know

where am I taking you?' Then in Serbian he says, 'Back
to where you belong.'

He pats me on the cheek and motions for both of us
to get back in the van. Before he closes the door on us,
he says with a glassy smile, 'Time to eat. We'll be there
soon.' We are each given a large baguette with limp lettuce
escaping from either end.

I haven't realised how hungry I am. Suddenly nothing
else matters.

Later on I'm feeling a bit better: we've got the torch
they left in the van. I'm clean and fed and listening to the
hum of heavy traffic on either side of us. I sneak a look
at Joe. And because nothing outside of here makes sense
any more, that's all the world is about: him and me, and
his brown eyes in the torchlight. And because I'm feeling
reckless or stupid or because nothing really matters any
more, I say:

'Joe?'

Straight away he says, 'Don't say sorry.'

I laugh, 'I'm not going to.'

I was. I was going to start with that.

'What then?'

It comes out then: 'You know Camille?'

There's a long pause then he says, 'I … we're not
together any more. I mean, I don't know if you knew, we
used to go out.'

I reckon along with everyone in the school, there's
probably a family of moles living under the football pitch
that knows Joe and Camille were going out.

'I ... saw you with her. And Zoe. They seemed ... you seemed ...'

'When?'

'At school,' I say miserably.

'Oh. Yeah. That. Listen I can't help it if she comes over and acts like that.' He pauses and pushes his hair off his face.

'I was just wondering ... why did you and Camille finish? I mean ... you don't have to tell me if you don't want to. I'm ... *shit* ... I'm sorry.'

'No. It's OK. I finished with her because I found out she was seeing James behind my back. I walked in on them and you know ... I ... She was all over me: *'I'm sorry, it was James, he wouldn't leave me alone, it doesn't mean anything...'* and you know what, I was thinking I should hit him, but watching her there in front of the two of us, trying to get out of it, I could see he was gutted. She'd obviously lied to him as well – told him he was the one – the same old crap.'

'I had no idea.'

'That's OK. I'm over it.'

'She's ... she's really beautiful.'

He stares at me for the longest time, then looks away. 'Yeah. Yeah, maybe. I used to think so. But I can't see it any more. I guess it's because I know how much she knows it. How much she uses it.'

'Is ... um ... are you ... is Zoe ...?'

'What about Zoe?'

'Um ...'

We run over a bump in the road and a pair of table legs bound with duct tape falls onto the floor beside me.

'I don't even like Zoe,' he says, then, 'so what about you and boys? I never knew – were you going out with anyone?'

I splutter. 'Boys? No. Not. Boys. I don't really have that many friends. Well … I have one friend – Lauren,' I trail off into a mumble.

'So you see people outside of school?'

'No,' I say.

I swallow.

He looks down and plays with the buttons on the torch. The heavy stench of diesel is filling my lungs like wet wool.

He says, 'Why?'

'Why what?'

'Why no friends?'

I take a deep breath: 'Because I'm just one of those people who don't. I'm not … popular. I don't know how to *be*. I can never seem to think of what to say, you know? I can't be funny or clever. I'm shy. I'm really, really shy. I mean, I don't make it easy for people.'

'Is that what you think?'

'I know it. You're lucky.'

'Why d'you say that?'

'Well. It's obvious. I mean everyone likes you. You're … you know …'

'What?'

'Well, you're … I don't know, you're in a band, girls like you …'

He's watching me, an odd expression on his face. Then he says, 'Bullshit. Being in a band doesn't mean I'm popular. I just like playing music. Any fans we have – and we don't have that many – all like the lead singer. And, yeah, I've been out with girls: two girls, two relationships, and they both cheated on me. So who's popular now?'

'I don't understand.'

'What's not to understand? Being shy isn't an incurable disease. You can get over it. Maybe I hang out with more people than you do, but I'm shy too. If it comes to that I reckon most people are. Some of us just work at it a bit harder.'

'I guess.'

He hesitates. I sense his eyes on me. He says, 'Have you *ever* had a boyfriend?'

I feel the blood rush to the surface of my skin and I'm glad we're sitting in semi darkness. I wait a while before answering.

'No. That's why I didn't believe you when …' I look at him. A quick glance and away again, but he catches it.

He sits up against the side of the van.

'Look. I asked you out because I like you. Because I wanted to get to know you better. It's not that complicated. I mean, it happens all the time.'

'Not to me it doesn't.'

'That's because you don't look like you want it to. The thing is – you think you're shy but really you always look like you've got better things to be doing – like you're really independent.'

I'm dumbfounded. *Independent?* 'But I'm a loser, Joe – I'm shy, I'm clumsy – people laugh at me. I don't understand.'

He's smiling. 'Sanda, you're not a loser. You might think you are – that's not what other people think.'

'Other people? Other people don't notice me.'

'Other people notice you – take it from me.'

'In a good way?'

'In a good way.'

I roll over on the blanket. I need to think. He says nothing but sits and fiddles with the torch, switching it on and off like some weird signal. And I see myself like I'm looking through two different lenses: the me lens where I'm a nobody, and the other lens where I'm not: where I'm independent, confident, with – what had he said? – better things to do. Come to think of it, Lauren had said it too. And no matter how I try, I can't get the lenses to close together to become one. It makes me think about my life with my parents and how seeming and being can be two completely different things.

Joe breaks the silence. 'Are you OK?'

'Yeah,' I breathe.

I decide that I'll keep this conversation and look at it later. I turn to the matter in hand: the small matter of being kidnapped.

8

We lie in silence for a while and I can hear him breathing softly. My mind's whirring. I raise myself up onto my elbow and turn to him.

'Did *you* get an idea of where we might be going? Did they say anything?'

He's kind enough to play along. 'Plenty. But all in their language. Sanda, I have no idea. I mean we're going east but you figured that anyway.'

'Yeah. Yeah. But …' I can still see Andrija's face in mine: sour breath and purple flesh.

'But what?'

'I don't know. Just something he said, about where we were going …'

'Go on.'

'"*Back to where you belong*" – that's what he said.'

He breathes out and it's almost a whistle, and somehow the air thickens and curdles. I know he's thinking what I'm thinking: about what it might mean.

After a minute, he says, 'But your parents?'

'What about them? He's right. They didn't want me. They don't want me.'

'Don't talk like that. Maybe they had to go because they owed money or something? The mortgage?'

'Oh yeah. Of course. The mortgage. The gas bill was overdue so they just emptied the house and pissed off without me.' I'm being a bitch. 'Sorry,' I say. He smiles and I go on, 'I've been thinking about it. I think they're in trouble. I think in the past they did something – or *saw* something – really bad and maybe whatever it is has finally caught up with them.'

'What sort of thing?'

I roll over and pull the newspaper cutting from my pocket. I wait a moment before handing it to him.

He squints at the paper in the torchlight. 'Who are all these men? Soldiers?'

'I think so. That one's my dad.'

'Yeah? What was he, like a mercenary?'

'I don't know.'

'What does it say?'

'This bit says Scorpions. I don't know why, or what it means. The rest is just a list of names. But I can't find his name there.'

'So maybe it's not him?'

'It's him. It's just a different name.'

'Where did you find it?'

'In the attic at home. That's where I was when you called me.'

Again I feel that bleakness overwhelm me in a kind of icy embrace.

'You don't look like him – your dad,' he says.

'I know.'

'Do you look like your mum?'

'No.'

He looks at me and I can see that he's wrestling with whether to ask the question: the one I've locked up in a drawer deep in the back of my mind.

I cut in: 'You live with your mum, don't you?'

He's quiet for a moment. 'Um … yeah. Sometimes, yeah.'

'Sometimes?'

'She stays away sometimes. Men. I'm on my own a lot, I mean I manage. It's not a problem.'

'So where's –?'

'My dad?'

'Yeah. Do you see him … much of him?'

'He lives in Germany. He's married with a baby.'

'Oh right.'

'I see him about twice a year when he comes over.'

'Oh.'

He shifts position and I catch something in his eyes that I haven't seen before.

'When he comes over, he stays with us and they always get drunk and end up in bed together and they seem to think that's not going to be a head-fuck for me at all. I know they're adults and there's no law against it but I can't get my head round the fact that Dad's got a kid back in

Germany and he's cheating on his wife with his ex-wife. But last time he was here he took me to Wembley to see England play.'

'So was that OK? The football?'

'I hate football. And he knows it, but he's a big Arsenal fan. He left after that – went straight to the airport – and I spent the evening with Mum in tears because she's still in love with him. Classy guy.'

'I had no idea.'

'How could you? No one does. I don't talk about it.'

'I'm sorry.'

'You're doing it again.'

'What?'

'Saying sorry.'

I smile and look down. 'Busted.'

'Actually it's good to talk about it – makes it seem more normal. Anyway you changed the subject. We were talking about *your* parents. What do you think is going on?'

'I wondered …'

'What?'

'Well, I guess when something like this happens, when everyone you thought you knew turns out to be not what you thought at all, then maybe that means I'm not what I thought at all either.'

'You're not making sense.'

'If my parents aren't who I thought they were; if they were – I don't know – pretending, then what does that make me?' I wait. 'D'you see where I'm going?'

'If I'm honest, not really,' he says.

I breathe, 'I'm just starting to wonder if … if I'm their daughter at all. You know, if everything else is messed up, if everything else is a lie, then why not that?'

'So you think …?'

'I don't know. In some ways it would really make a lot of things clear. Although why would you adopt a child you didn't want or even like?'

'Why? Is that what they were like? Shit Sanda. That's rough.'

His voice and the kindness in it make me want to cry again. Quickly I hand over the photograph, the one of the child.

'This was all they left.'

He takes it and turns it over in his hands. He looks at it for a long time without speaking then he says, 'Is this you?' I nod. 'But the name on the back, who's that?'

'Senka. Senka Hadžić. That's my grandmother's name apparently; at least that's what my dad told me.'

'You don't believe him?'

I shake my head. 'They've done this to me. They've lied to me. Why should anything be true any more?'

He nods gravely and hands back the photograph, and I think about those bone fragments of memories of my childhood and they're dust. White ash.

'You know, you can find out if you're … adopted. They have to tell you.'

I look at him. 'Maybe.'

'What is it?' he says.

'I'm just thinking, if I was adopted — and this is me in the photo — and my Dad was some kind of soldier in the war there …'

'What war?'

'In the early nineties there was a war in Bosnia … you must know that.'

'I heard something about it maybe …'

'Well, there was a war — it started in 1992. The Bosnian Serbs wanted an independent Serbia.'

'Who won?'

'Who won? My God. That's so like a boy.'

'Well — it's important, isn't it?'

'Everyone and no one. They just made peace I think.'

'OK. So, maybe you were an orphan. Maybe your real parents were killed in the war and your dad — I mean your adopted dad — found you and adopted you?'

'God, I really need to know.'

'So who's this Branko then? If they think I'm helping you for him, then … well, he *must* be someone you know.'

'I don't know anyone called Branko.'

'You *sure?*'

'*Yes.* Maybe they were confused. Or making it up.'

Joe looks away.

Just then the van slows and brakes and Joe drops the torch, which goes out. I hear a fist banging on the side and the doors open.

'OK, get out,' says Andrija.

We're in a fenced car park with trucks and trailers all around us. In the toilet block, I wash my face and smooth my hair. Once we're back in the van, they give us sandwiches and water. We start up the torch again and try to settle down. Joe is asleep at once but, exhausted as I am, it's a long time before I can go to sleep, and several times in the night, I wake to see the torchlight flickering and dying as the battery gives out.

Early in the morning, they wake us and the sandwich and toilet routine is repeated. We cross two borders in one day. I know, because before the crossing points, we're bound and gagged. At one border, the doors are opened and a torch flashed over the van contents. I even see the face of the border guard, heavy set with a black moustache. I chew and spit at the foul-tasting cotton gag to make some sound.

The next time we're allowed out, we're in Austria.

I can taste blood in my mouth.

We sleep then till we're woken by the van bumping and rolling over ground that doesn't feel like road, and when it comes to a halt and the doors are opened, it's dark. We're led out into a grassy clearing surrounded by tall spruce trees. Andrija gives us a bag of crisps each and we tear into them. I can hear water in the distance, and strange bird calls sound in the cold night air. Joe takes a blanket from the van and puts it round my shoulders.

Andrija and Boris pace about the clearing talking in low voices. Boris carries a rifle. Andrija tries his phone a couple of times. I find myself wondering whether he knows much more than we do.

I can't stop thinking about dying here in the forest, imagining falling onto the hard brush, my blood leeching away into the pine needles, my eyes open and staring. I shiver and all I can hear are my teeth drumming in my head.

The thing is I've never kissed a boy. And the boy I've dreamed about kissing practically every day since I first saw him is standing right next to me; except he might as well be a million miles away.

I turn to him in the oily darkness but he's looking straight ahead. I follow his gaze. Headlights strobe through the trees. A very old and battered Range Rover comes into view. The sides are pocked with holes and one of the back windows is shattered. I force myself to breathe.

9

Two people get out of the car. The first is a big woman – broad rather than fat. She has a man's body: barrel chest, wide back and sturdy legs. She looks old although her hair in the headlights shines bright orange. She wears a fur coat that looks like it's taken about a thousand small mammals to make. Her companion is tall with a shaved head. He's wearing a camouflage jacket and army boots.

A long and heated conversation follows. They're talking about Joe and how he wasn't part of the plan. They speak quietly but I'm sure I hear the word 'Branko'. All the while Boris is pointing the rifle at us in a rather half-hearted way.

My mouth is stale and my stomach boils. I put my hand out to Joe and he takes it, locking his fingers through mine. His eyes are steady.

Eventually Andrija and the woman come over to us. She folds her arms and her mouth is set while he speaks.

'This is Madame Milanković. She is … she will take you.'

'Where I belong'. Is this where I belong?

'What's going on?' I say. Joe is still as a rock but I feel the blood thumping in his wrist. I say in Serbian, 'We're not going anywhere until you tell us what you're doing. You can't do this.'

Andrija mutters something which I don't catch, then turns away and spits on the ground.

'Mirko, put them in the car,' says Milanković. The tall man steps towards me. Joe gets between us and rams him in the chest with both hands.

'Run, Sanda!'

We crash though the undergrowth but we don't get far. Boris catches him across the back with the butt of the rifle and he sprawls headlong onto the ground.

'Joe!'

I stop and I go to him but Mirko gets there first. He sweeps him up in one powerful motion and carries him to the Range Rover. I try to follow but Milanković has me kneeling in front of her with one hand pressing vice-like on my neck and her knee in my back.

I see Andrija and Boris hovering uncertainly until Milanković says, 'You can go.' Boris shuffles off and climbs into the cab.

Andrija hesitates a moment, looks back at me, scuffs the ground with his boot and leaves.

As the tail lights of the van disappear through the brush, I see Mirko striding towards me from the car. He reaches me quickly and heaves me over his shoulder.

I start screaming. I'm screaming and it's like someone else is doing it. It's like I'm outside my body and floating high above the forest, listening to the sound tearing up into space.

Mirko opens the car door and tosses me in. I plummet back down to earth.

Joe raises his head, his eyes half closed. He reaches out, finds my hand and grips it. And then I'm quiet again. He sinks back against the seat.

We're going at speed through pine forests, over dirt tracks, past tiny hamlets, tumbledown houses with broken roofs; I see snow-frosted mountains way in the distance. We're thrown together then apart as the car careers round sharp bends. We make our way up and up, and the gears squeal and crunch as we skid on. Joe's head is lolling forward, and every so often he emits an ugly groan. From time to time, Milanković snaps at Mirko who grunts assent.

Then, with the moon high in a black night sky, we turn a corner and pull up through iron gates into a steep drive.

Ahead of us rises a kind of castle: tall grey turrets with evil little windows squinting down at us; steps up to a great door. The windows on the first two floors have bars on them. A large sign is bolted to the gatepost: *Zbrisč Sirotište*. A ringing starts up in my head because I've heard the word *sirotište* but I can't place it. I'm still thinking about it when I catch sight of a child at a ground-floor window. His head is shaved and he watches the car with wide, dark eyes in his pinched face. As the iron gates clang shut behind us, the meaning comes to me: *orphanage*.

The car has child locks so we have to wait to be let out.

I can tell Joe's as scared as I am; I can see the muscles in his forearms tightening and his fists round on his thighs.

'It's OK,' I say. 'They'll let you go now.'

'I don't think so,' he says, 'I think they want both of us.'

The door on my side is opened by Mirko. Milanković waits in the car while I'm hauled out onto the ground. He yanks me up and frogmarches me towards the door. I'm kicking and hitting at him for all I'm worth and yelling Joe's name. All I hear are Joe's muffled shouts and an impotent thumping on the windows of the car.

In minutes we're inside. I hear footsteps hurrying over flagstones. Mirko lets go of me and dusts himself off. Again footsteps, but different: a fat slap of rubber this time and a figure comes into view. A thin woman with bleached hair piled up in a beehive. She wears overalls and rubber boots like she works on a farm. She takes hold of my arm while chatting to Mirko.

After a minute, they exchange a curt good bye and she steers me away down a shadowy corridor.

She takes me to a concrete cell with a low arched ceiling and bolts the door behind us. The room smells of bleach and is lit by a single bulb. At one end, is a tiled section of floor and wall and at the other, a table and two chairs. On the table is a small brown parcel tied with string.

She says nothing. She sits at the table, crosses her legs and gestures to me by plucking at her clothes that she wants me to strip. In spite of the cold, I'm burning. I want to refuse but I can see it's pointless. I make up my mind I won't cry. Slowly I bend to untie my shoelaces as she touches up her lipstick. The floor is wet and there's nowhere dry to put my clothes. I leave them in a heap, carefully tucking the photograph and cutting I've carried from London inside a sleeve. I stand there in my bra and pants, shivering and rubbing my arms, my flesh blue and goose pimpled.

She looks up then and comes around the table to face me.

'Everything,' she says. She waits while I peel off my underwear. I must not cry. I must not cry. I fold my arms across my body and shuffle back towards the tiled wall. She twists me around to face the wall with my palms flat against it.

And then water. Cold water: a force like I've never known pummels my back and legs. She shouts at me to turn, and holding my arms across myself to protect my frozen body I do as she orders. She grips the hose in both hands and the icy jet rams against my face and nearly knocks me off balance. I brace myself against the wall to stop myself falling.

Just as suddenly, the water is switched off; she throws me a towel and I start to rub myself dry.

She opens the package on the table to reveal a set of clothes and motions to me to put them on. I ignore her. I'm dry now.

I wind the towel around me and I say: 'Where's my friend? *Where's my friend?* I want to see him.'

Her mouth contorts into a sneer. 'You'll find out soon enough.'

Rage surges through me and I spit at her. Time slows and in the moment of peace before she hits me, I watch the bubbles of my saliva crawling down her rouged cheek. Her lips are slightly parted and a curl of spit licks its way into her mouth. She snaps her mouth shut.

The blow lands hard on my face. She shakes her hand a few times as though to soothe the sting. Something in me, some small defiant part of me, gives me the strength to hold my ground. I meet her gaze and again, very calmly this time, I ask, 'Where is my friend? What have you done with him?'

She curses in response and goes out, locking the door behind her.

I take out the clothes. They consist of a garish collection of hand-me-downs that smell of stale dishtowels: flared cords, boots, a knitted jumper with a zip, a T-shirt that says *'University of Michigan'* on it, and a pair of men's socks. I gather up the cuttings and stuff them into the pocket of the cords.

The woman returns with a large pair of blunt scissors and cuts off my hair. And when it's done, she steps back and looks at me in an odd way as though she's about to say something but then thinks better of it. She goes to the door, beckons me. I pick up the little bundle of my old clothing and follow her down dimly lit corridors with doors opening off them into wide rooms like hospital wards or dormitories, full of beds packed tightly together. Many of the rooms are lit by candles, and I can just make out indistinct shapes huddled on beds and in corners.

Every nerve in my body, every cell, is like a lit match, fizzing and spitting.

Everywhere the floors are wood or stone and the high ceilings make the place almost as cold as the outside. The walls are bare and giant hides of peeling paint spiral away from them. In places there are even holes like some massive fist has punched through from the outside, and the freezing wind saws in as we pass. I stop at a mottled mirror and I don't recognise the person staring back at me: my hair stands up in tufts, bits she's missed hang down around my ears, my face looks thin and drawn and there are dark purple shadows under my eyes. My parents have done this to me. *My family.*

Finally I'm locked in a room and left to sleep on a thin mattress. I wake at dawn and lie there watching the dust motes glittering like beads in the light.

I need to get away as soon as possible, to find Joe and get out. Because of all I've lost, somehow losing Joe, and the kind of *idea* of Joe, matters more than anything. Where nothing is sure any more, where everything that means something turns out to be false or compromised, Joe is real. Now they've taken him too.

Later, I'm sitting on a rickety child's chair outside what looks like an office. I'm with the beehive woman from last night who knocks at the door. She looks nervous. The door opens and she drags me into the room where Milanković is standing waiting. The office is a complete contrast to what is outside it. The floor is carpeted, a lamp gives out a soft glow, and there are curtains rather than bars at the window, a huge pink cabbage print that Mum would have loved.

Milanković goes to her chair and plumps the cushions before she sits down. On her desk is a plate of assorted chocolate biscuits. I notice a couple have been nibbled and put back.

She smiles and on her teeth I see traces of chocolate.

She says in Serbian, 'Sanda. Welcome to Zbrisć.'

'Where's my friend? What have you done with him?' I try not to raise my voice.

'Your *friend*.' She says the word carefully, rolls it in her mouth. 'He's safe.'

'What am I doing here? You can't keep me here. I want to see him.'

'You are going to stay here for a while Sanda, so you need to behave yourself. We do not like bad behaviour at Zbrisć.'

'*What for?* Why am I here?'

'This – this is bad behaviour, asking questions all the time.'

'Look, I'll behave when you tell me where my friend is and where my parents are and why you're keeping me here.'

She runs her pink tongue around her lips, hoovering up biscuit crumbs like a snake. 'Your parents are in the country.'

'Can I see them?'

'No. Not now. Not yet.'

'Where's Joe?'

She shakes her head slowly and reaches into a drawer for a packet of cigarettes. 'No.'

'What does that mean, *no*? I want to know where you've taken him.'

She settles into her chair and eyes me with interest; lights a cigarette and sits back in a curl of smoke.

'They were right. You are trouble.'

'They spoke to you? About me?'

She shrugs. 'It's easy. You will stay here and you will behave yourself. That's all. No more questions.'

I start to protest but she waves me away and I'm shunted out of the room to the sound of her coughing.

I cannot process what is happening to me. I cannot see in front of me or behind me.

The woman says, 'Come with me.'

We go back down the corridor and stop at a large doorway to a kind of dining room. It's like the school lunch hall, only not. For a start, it's freezing. At the opposite end on the outside wall, a gaping hole lets in a rush of icy wind. Someone has tried to patch it with bits of floorboards nailed across it and what look like bin bags. On top of the sour smell of shit that follows us everywhere, there's a smell of rotting meat and vegetables.

Something runs across the floor in front of us as we move towards the smell: a rat.

It's the first time I get to see some of my fellow inmates. All girls, in various states of undress, and it's difficult to tell the age of most of them. All of them are quiet apart from the odd squeak or howl. They queue at a counter where two women in head scarves and filthy aprons dole out the bread, and they move forward with their eyes fixed on their feet.

As soon as the girls are given their bread, they squirrel it under their arms and carry it away like a precious bundle. I'm pushed into the queue and they move back to accommodate me. Other than that, no one seems particularly interested in me.

The person in front of me is behaving strangely – now and again spasms run through her body and her arms shake. She's finding it hard to take the bread they offer and I realise they're teasing her. The larger of the two women holds out the bread, waits for her to compose herself enough to get it and then pulls it away again. They shriek with laughter as the poor girl tries to grab the food.

Then I hear her say softly, '*Molim?* Please?'

There's so much sadness and dignity and humanness in those words. On an impulse, I snatch the bread from the old witch and give it to the girl. She looks at me and for a second I see the person she might have been. She's small but I figure she's about my age. A shock of short dark hair and violet eyes. She shuffles away quickly to eat the bread. I watch her go and move up to the counter. The crones are furious. One takes the bread intended for me and with fleshy fingers, she breaks it in two. Half rations.

As I take it, I look her straight in the eye and say, 'It was worth it.'

I turn and walk over to one of the high windows that line the wall making the room even colder. I want to see what I'm up against and how hard it would be to escape. As I bite into the dense earthy hunk of bread, I look down through the bars on the yard below: beyond the high wire perimeter fence, there are pine forests, and way off in the distance, snowy mountains. It's a clear day and the peaks sparkle in the high wintry sun. It gives me a sort of hope that there is a world outside where I might be wanted after all.

In the yard, there are a couple of mangy dogs tethered to a concrete post near the fence and a small outbuilding with a lightning sign on it in white paint which I guess to be the generator for the orphanage. As I watch, a young boy struggles across the yard. He's carrying two buckets that look almost as big as him and probably weigh more than he does. I'm struck, firstly, by the fact that he's wearing flip-flops and the temperature outside, if the temperature inside is anything to go by, must be around freezing; and secondly, by the fact that he's a boy which means there are boys here. Which means Joe may still be here, still close. Lost in thought, I chew on the bread.

Someone pinches me gently on the elbow and brings me back into the room. The girl I helped at the counter is standing next to me. In her hand she holds part of her bread. She points to me and gently gives me the bread, like some kind of religious offering, then steps back and watches me with red-rimmed eyes. I know what it means.

She's probably hungrier than I'll ever be. The bread is life or death to her and she's giving up half of it for me. And that gesture, like the sun on the snow, like thinking of Joe out there, gives me hope. My eyes fill with tears and I nod to her,

'*Hvala.* Thank you'

10

The girl smiles and it transforms her. She studies me intently, says something under her breath, and then I realise she's noticed my odd eyes.

I smile back and point to my chest: 'Sanda,' I say, 'My name is Sanda.'

She seems puzzled and hesitates a while, as though she's trying to remember something. Then, quietly, almost in a whisper: 'I'm Andjela'

'Andjela,' I repeat.

I take her hand. It's cold and sticky and bare as bone.

I'm facing the door and I see a warder striding towards us. Quickly, I shove the bread back at her and turn away to the window. I look back to see my new friend being hustled out of the room, cowering and shaking as before. I go after her but I'm stopped at the door by another warder.

Soon after that, a bell rings. I take up my place again by the window and watch the weary procession of kids, old and young, file out of the room. Afterwards, I hear the sounds of doors locking and unlocking, and the odd strangled cry that seems to be part of the ugly music of this place.

I want to see Andjela again. We've made a connection – it's not much but it's something. I look over at the kitchen staff in the back behind the counter, and I see one of them, the one who tormented Andjela, stuffing her face with a large pastry.

As I go to leave, I spy a small loaf left on a table. I snatch it up and stuff it under my top. One of the warders comes in then and calls me out into the corridor.

I'm shown into a room with high arched windows. There are perhaps twenty beds with rusting frames, all occupied by girls of varying ages. The girls watch me with unblinking eyes. One scratches herself constantly, her arms and legs red and blistered.

I close my arms around my body just to feel I have a body. Skin and bones. Elbows and knees. I need to remember who I am. Then I find my voice:

'Andjela? Where's Andjela?'

No one responds. In the nearest bed, a small girl clutches her knees up to her chest and rocks back and forth. I offer the bread I've stolen from the kitchen. She flashes her eyes at me and grabs it.

I say, 'Where is Andjela?'

I wait while she eats. I can see the bread mashed into dough in her mouth. She jabs a finger in the direction of another door at the end of the room.

This leads to another dormitory: the door to the

corridor is closed and there are shutters at the windows. In the feeble light, I can just make out a coil of bodies on a corner bed. One of them raises her head as I enter. Even in the gloom I recognise her at once.

I cross to the window and gesture for her to join me. After a pause, she comes over. Under little rakes of light that seep through the shutters, I ask her in Serbian, 'Are you OK? I was worried.'

She stiffens. Her eyes dart up at me and then over to the door. 'Yes, yes, I'm all right.'

'Andjela,' I say, 'it's OK. I'm your friend. I'm not going to hurt you.'

She looks at me carefully and then says slowly, 'Who *are* you?'

'What do you mean?'

She's about to say something more when the door is opened abruptly and a long shadow is cast across the floor. She slides down against the wall and covers her head.

Right then, I decide that when we get out of here, she's coming with us. But first, I need to find Joe. I need to get into the boys' block, and to do that I need to get outside. I'm going to have to be patient.

I spend the days that follow waiting for my chance. I watch the yard, the gates and the fence all the time. I think about home and Mum and Dad; about me: what I was, what I am and what I might be.

And I think about Joe.

I think about our journey here, what we said to each other, what he did for me and what he was for me, and

...ery word and every look and I fold them into myself until they're part of me and he's part of me.

It's weird, but in this place that seems so closed and hopeless, I have found a sort of hope. Maybe it's the freedom that comes with being locked up: when nothing seems possible, in a way everything is.

Andjela and I see a lot of each other. I move myself into her dormitory and no one seems to mind. I make sure always to save a little food for her. As a way of passing the time, I'm teaching her to speak some English. I scratch out a picture on the wall and I say the English word and she says it after me. Late at night, lying restless in my cot, I hear her softly sounding the words like a mantra in the cold room: 'Boy. Girl. Me. You. Mother. Father. Brother. Sister. Friend. Friend. Friend.'

One day I draw a picture of two girls holding hands, both thin with spiky hair and round eyes. I write our names in charcoal over the images. I clasp my hands together and say, 'Friends.'

'Friends.' She touches my face with timid fingertips, draws back and points at my eyes.

'Eyes,' I say, *'oči.'*

'Eyes.' She looks at me intently and says, 'Sister.'

'No. Friend, Andjela. Not Sister.'

'Sister,' she repeats. She gently takes the charcoal from my hand, and draws another figure on the wall.

She indicates the eyes on the figure and says it again: *'Sister.'*

11

Before we have a chance to talk further, one of the warders comes into the room, looks about her and summons me to follow her. I get to my feet, leaving Andjela kneeling by the little charcoal pictures of the three girls.

I'm taken to the kitchen, given a rusting peeler and sat on a low stool beside a mountain of potatoes and a giant pot. My fingers struggle with the blunt instrument and large potatoes are reduced to marble-sized balls with most of the potato staying on the inside of the peel. From time to time, one of the kitchen staff leaves her gossiping at the counter, and comes and stands over me with her arms folded. I ignore them and eventually the job is done. My fingers are bleeding and my back is sore but I'm pleased with my efforts. I also manage to pilfer two little cakes that have been thrown away. I'm just thinking about how I'll give them to Andjela when one of the women shambles over and motions to the door.

She picks up the enormous bucket of peelings in her red hands and gives it to me. I stagger under its weight towards the door. On the other side of the yard, I see two huge bins under a wooden lean-to. I need no further instruction, and, sliding in my boots on the icy ground, I pitch out with the bucket. One of the dogs looks up with lazy eyes as I approach.

It's the first time I've been outside since the night we were handed over, and it feels good to breathe clean air after the rank stew inside. I dump the bucket and begin slowly transferring the waste into the nearest container. The bins are nearly full and there's a light crusting of frost over the evil mulch inside. I startle at cawing overhead. Five crows land around me working their frayed wings and pecking at the ground waiting for me to leave.

I glance back at the kitchen. No one's watching me. Looking up at the third floor, I'm pretty sure I can locate the window of the refectory where I first saw the boy. I'm standing exactly where he was and now I can see where he was going. There's another wing of the building that I hadn't seen before.

Checking behind me to make sure I'm not being watched, I take a sharp breath, pick up my bucket and stride purposefully towards the new block.

A door to the side of the block opens easily and I go in. The stench is overpowering, stronger than where we are. I almost gag and have to put my head outside and gulp in a breath.

Back inside, I take stock: the room is long and narrow with an arched ceiling. There are benches and tables stacked to the sides. There's a door at the end.

The place is silent.

I force myself on, crossing the flags quietly, and try the door. It leads onto a corridor with small doors set in the walls. All are bolted shut. At the end, there's a short flight of stairs which takes me to the first floor and more rooms. I keep on, head down, holding up the potato bucket at my chest, hoping that no one stops me. No one does. The place seems empty of warders. A small barefooted boy approaches, peers hopefully into the bucket and melts back into the walls. As I go, I call Joe's name softly.

In the last room, I'm answered, a hoarse voice through the fug:

'What?'

I start at the sound. As I peer into the murk, a familiar form materialises. I know him at once. I put down my bin and go to him. I try to hold him, to find him again. He smells sour, seems thinner. I can feel the grid of bones in his chest. He stands very still when I hold him, and his heart beats like a bird when you catch it.

'It's so, so, so good to see you! I thought – I thought … Oh fuck Joe. I'm so sorry. This is all my fault.'

He looks down at me. His head's shaved. He's still Joe and yet altered. He shakes me off roughly, stands back and glares at me. I'm too shocked to be hurt. Then I realise we're not alone: ghostly figures leave the walls and crowd in on us. I push the bin at them and they scrabble for the few potato scraps left there.

'Joe? *Joe?* Talk to me.' His eyes are hard. 'What is it? Joe, please?'

'*Now* you want to talk? I don't understand you, Sanda. What's going on? You ignore me for days and then you rush in like you haven't seen me since they left us.'

'What do you mean? What are you talking about?' I say.

'Are you playing games with me? Are you *deliberately* trying to fuck with me?'

'Joe, this *is* the first time I've seen you since they left us.'

'Right.'

'Joe, please?'

He relaxes slightly and frowns. 'You've been here every day Sanda. I've seen you cleaning up, doling out food. I called you and called you. I stood there like a fucking idiot calling your name and you didn't even look up. I went right up to you and you looked straight through me.'

I'm baffled. He has tears in his eyes and I know he means every word. I take his hands and I fold them over mine.

'Joe, this is the first time I've seen you since that night. It's the first time I've been out of the girls' block. I've been trying to find out where they took you. You *have* to believe me ... *why on earth would I ignore you?*'

He brushes a slug of snot from his nose and wipes his eyes, shakes his head. 'She was just like you. She had eyes like yours.'

'Well, I know it's unusual but I'm not the only one in the world with odd eyes. Joe, it wasn't me, I promise. How could it have been? Believe me.'

He shrugs and looks away. 'Whatever.'

'Joe?' And I say because I can't not say it: 'We have to get out of here. We … I can't … I'm losing it Joe …'

He looks at me then and nods slowly. 'I know. But it's so weird. They really think I'm working for this Branko. They're trying to get me to tell them what I know, where he is. I keep telling them I don't know what they're talking about.'

'Your mum will have gone to the police by now.'

'She won't have noticed I'm gone. It was half-term wasn't it? She'll think I'm staying at a mate's. If you're pinning your hopes on her, you're going to be disappointed.'

'I'm sorry.'

'It's OK.'

'That woman said something about me *waiting* here. Like something's going to happen soon.'

'Waiting?'

'Doesn't sound good, does it?'

He hangs his head. 'No. And once they realise I'm telling the truth and I've got nothing they want, then I'm toast, and you – I thought you were – I thought they were going to …'

'Don't,' I whisper. Gently I take his arm and pull him back with me against the wall where we're in shadow. 'All we have to do right now is get out.'

He shrugs and I pinch his arm. 'Joe?'

He studies me for a while and then a kind of smile lifts his face. 'OK. OK. What's the plan?'

'Well I don't have one. I didn't know I was even going to find you here.'

'Well ...' he says, 'the fence. Have you seen the fence?'

'Yeah, it goes all round,' I say. 'It's high and it looks pretty tight, what I've seen of it. Could we get under it?'

He folds his arms and leans back against the wall. 'Not without cutting it. It's set deep in the ground ... No. I don't think so.'

'What then ... just ... go over it?'

'I don't know. Maybe.'

'Yeah?' my voice cracks.

'Yeah ... yeah, I think so.' He ponders this for a moment. I can hear voices from below.

I say, 'When?'

'What?'

'When can we go?'

He stands up away from the wall. The voices are closer now.

'Tomorrow night. Late. After lights out. Meet me outside by the bins?'

'OK,' I say.

He says, 'It's going to be hard work, the fence. It won't be easy.'

That makes me think about Andjela. I don't know if *I'll* be able to do it let alone her. As I'm thinking about when and how to tell Joe about her, he does something so unexpected that it takes my breath away. He leans down and hooks a strand of hair from my stubby fringe that escaped the scissors. His touch still makes me blush, and in spite of the cold, I can feel my skin redden and tingle.

'Look after yourself,' he says and disappears. A man enters the room and speaks to me in Serbian, gesturing to the bin.

I say, *'Da, da.'*

I shoulder the bin and as I track back across the yard I stop for a moment to check out the fence. It's about twenty feet high and made of a dense mesh of thick wire. But there's enough room in the loops for hand and footholds. Just.

I tell Andjela about the plan. Calling it a *plan* makes it seem more realistic than it actually is. Right now, it's just a thing we're going to try. But as she watches me intently, I start to believe that, what the hell, it might just be possible. And I know she's coming with us. I know I can't leave her behind.

In the morning, we awake to water ringing against a tin bucket in the corridor. A fierce gale is blowing down from the mountain driving grey sheets of rain before it.

Later, I'm summoned to Milanković's office. As before, I wait on the tiny stool outside but this time she's not in her room. I hear her thighs in their thick orange tights squeaking against each other as she approaches.

She stops in front of me. 'Inside.'

She settles herself in her chair, lights up a cigarette and turns her small eyes on me. I wait. She coughs into her fist once, twice, and leans towards me over the table.

'I have something for you.'

Just then there's a knock at the door and she hoists herself out of her chair, making the wood creak and whine. It's one of the kitchen women and she's not happy about something. There's a short exchange and Milanković goes out, closing the door behind her saying, 'Wait.'

I stand still, listening to the rain drumming against the panes and the sound of voices rising and falling from behind the door. The desk is littered with her grubby leavings, like the nest of some outsized squirrel: biscuit crumbs, dead flowers, what looks like a pair of socks, a paper knife, and a jumble of thin cardboard files lying across the desk at odd angles.

At the top of each file is a small tin clip with a name on it. I don't know what makes me look, but I do. I crane forward to see better and my heart stops because near the bottom of the pile is one with a name I recognise, one I've carried with me from London: *Senka Hadžić*.

I can *feel* her hand on the door handle before I hear it, and, without thinking, I slide out the contents. I pull off the name tag and attach it to another file. I fold the papers and stuff them down my sock. When she comes back into the room, I'm there with my head bowed, waiting. Against my skin, the paper shifts and scratches and settles.

She sits down again and picks her teeth distractedly. I look up at her.

'Yes … yes. I have something. Your parents. Your father …'

It's not what I expect and it winds me. I manage, *'What?'*

She tugs at a drawer in her desk and takes out a piece of folded notepaper.

'A message. From your father.'

'He was here?'

She shakes her head. 'No.'

She holds it out to me, pinched between finger and thumb, and I reach for it slowly. The paper's been wet and it crackles in my hand as I open it. My father's scrawling hand in black ink that has run like tears down the page:

Sanda

When you are a child you are dreaming. Your eyes are shut.

When you are grown up you open your eyes.

You can see.

Life is complicated.

Everything is not what you think.

Nothing is what it seems.

I am very sorry, I should have done more but love is complicated too.

Goodbye.

Dragan.

I read it once and then again. And what I've carried with me for so long, that *blankness*, that quiet obedience just granulates and scatters on the floor. That there's someone who, in his way, *did* care about me, did think about me, is *sorry*, makes everything so much harder.

I suck the paper into my fist, and I run. All I can hear is the hammer of my feet on stone, on wood and on concrete. The ground rolling under me and the rain beating down. Then I'm outside where the walls lean and tower and the high windows watch me.

Two minutes on, there's a hand on my shoulder.

'Inside. *Now!*'

I let myself be taken into the kitchen where the two kitchen women snitch and sneer at me. Milanković's hair has all but collapsed in the rain, and one of them offers a filthy tea towel which she declines.

Instead, she picks through a bucket of kitchen implements until she finds what she's looking for: a sturdy wooden ladle. She brings it down on my head and sides and arms and I stumble and fall. I crouch with my arms over my head but she keeps hitting me. All I can see and hear and feel is pain. Pain like something is living inside me and pushing under my skin to get out. When I open my eyes, it's still raining but I can hear the crows again. I see her standing over me:

'You are spoiled stupid girl. You will learn how to behave.'

I'm learning fast.

12

I don't know how long I lie there, curled tight on the kitchen floor. Small things buzz in and out of my consciousness: cracked flagstones, the reek of cinder and fat from the ovens and the steady beat of rain on glass. Pain and heat all over my body. I push against the cold stone to ease it. Very slowly, I lift my head and through the grimy windows I see the mountains, and in the foreground, the fence.

The papers I took are still there, I can feel them chafe at my ankle.

Then there are fingers on my shoulders and a low murmuring, and I'm helped to my feet. It's Andjela. I find I can hardly stand. I lean against her and, hopping and limping, we make it upstairs. On the bed with my knees pulled into my chest, I let myself cry. She watches me with her head on one side like a curious starling, and after a while she leans in and opens her arms and pulls me into a bony embrace.

'Friend,' she whispers in English.

I return it: 'Friend.'

I lie back. She covers me with a blanket. A tent. A rind. A shield. I'm still breathing. I'm still here. I hear her footsteps die away across the floor and I'm alone. I think about my father, about what he wrote. Deep down, I always knew it: that whatever I had or thought I had was never quite *real*.

But this: this is real. And all that matters now is to get out, over the wire, to run from all this. And in spite of what's just happened I'm ready for it.

Andjela returns in a while with some soup and bread. She sits me up and watches me eat it. When I'm done, I stretch out my legs and look at myself. I roll up my trousers and my legs are black with bruises. My arms and sides too. They cover my body in dark blooms. We look at each other and her hand in mine is bent into a fist, hard as rock.

Later, much later, when the rooms are quiet and all I can hear is the hum of breathing, shallow and deep, and the occasional rustle or dreaming moan, we're ready.

Andjela has traded bread for two wool jackets, both unravelling at the sleeves, one for each of us. We work our way silently down the stairs and out towards the kitchens and the back door. The rain has got worse, the storm is directly overhead and repeated tails of lightning crosses the sky and illuminate our faces. I catch Andjela, pale as a ghost, mouth agape as I pull her on. A rat scuttles across our path in the darkness and for a moment its eyes are red pin points of light. The kitchens are bolted but Andjela shows me a small serving hatch in the refectory. It's only a little wider than a dinner plate but she manages to push herself through it, wriggling and squirming. She lets me in and we go to the back door.

It's padlocked.

We stand in the kitchen, watching the rain against the glass, searching the blackness beyond for Joe. Minutes pass and all I can hear is our breath. We don't talk. We don't look at each other.

And then: in the yard, I see him. An indistinct figure, hunched against the rain, waiting.

I start looking frantically in the drawers and tins for something, *anything*, that we can use to break the window or cut the chain on the padlock. Then there's an almighty crack of thunder close overhead and when I turn, I see Andjela holding the ladle that Milanković used on me. Behind her, the pane in the door is smashed, and all around her feet, glass glitters in the lightning glare.

At once the figure bolts. He's on us, peering through the broken glass.

It's not Joe.

He thrusts a hand through the hole in the glass and grabs Andjela by the neck. I see him, his hair lashed wet against his face, his eyes dark pits: Mirko. Still holding her around the neck, he hoists himself through the broken pane and into the room. When he stands in front of us, the skin on his arms is cut from wrist to elbow.

'You going somewhere?' he hisses. Andjela's jaw is reddening above his fist; she stays very still, her eyes wide.

'Let her go!' I say. Never taking his eyes off me, he pushes Andjela to the floor. She tries to twist away from him but it's hopeless. I'm frozen: I see his breath hang in the air over her; I see her staring eyes, her hands up clawing at his. I cast about for something to stop it, to stop him. All over the floor are shards of glass. I see one big enough behind him near the door, I take it up and I pitch it hard into his neck and wrench it out.

Everything stops. His hands are still around Andjela's throat, she's struggling to breathe, her face blue, and then there's a bulge under his skin, and a hot stream of blood shoots upward and spatters the ceiling. He lurches forward and falls on top of Andjela, a steady pulse of blood leaching from the wound. I kneel and push his bulk off her and roll her on to her side where she coughs and retches. Already I can hear the sound of voices from far above us.

We have to get out now.

I force Andjela to her feet, turn her to face me. 'Ready?'

She nods quickly. We crouch down and I crawl to the broken door with her close at my heels. I can hear footsteps in the corridor leading to the refectory, the faint clink of keys.

I ease myself through what remains of the door, sharp little teeth of glass snatching at my arms and sides, turn and help Andjela, then through the boiling storm we dash towards the shelter of the bins and wait.

There's no sign of Joe.

A light is turned on in the kitchen and a cry goes up.

'Come on!' I look around in panic and there's someone there right in front of me. At once, I raise my hand in defence but he checks me, holds me. It's Joe.

'Where have you been?' I cry.

'There was a guy out there, I had to wait …'

Mirko: the glass in my fist. In his flesh. Blood high on the walls.

'Who's this?' Joe says, looking at Andjela.

'She's my friend,' I say and her eyes are on me, sharp as vinegar. 'She's coming with us.'

Over in the kitchen, it appears to be quiet, but then the slow whine of the alarm sounding. It gets louder and louder, screaming against the night.

Joe says, 'Come on.'

We run for it.

The rain is horizontal, whipping at our faces. We get to the fence and suddenly it looks so much taller than it did before. It towers above us, a criss-cross of gunmetal wire. I stare up at it in horror until Joe gives me a gentle push and says, 'Climb!'

To my left, Andjela has already kicked off her shoes, thrown them over the fence into the dense forest beyond and she's climbing, her white fingers clawing at the metal, and her hair, a dark liquid. I keep my boots on – the papers still tucked inside them – and grip the wet mesh. I haul myself up after Joe. He's already a few feet above me. The pain in my side bites as I reach upwards, and the wire digs into my hands.

Joe calls out, 'Don't look down! Come on Sanda!'

Inch by inch, we leave the ground behind us and

crawl up like insects. Thunder slices the air, and I feel I'm climbing into it: into the sky. I look back at the buildings. I'm level with the first floor now. At that moment, a sheet of lightning illuminates the brickwork. That's when I see the face, framed in a ground-floor window and lit for seconds by the glow. Watching us. No. Watching me. Her face. My face. She has *my* face: a shock of short hair, pale skin, a pointed chin. *I am seeing myself.* She puts up a hand in a kind of salute. A smile and she vanishes.

I hang there, my boots slipping and sliding on the wire. I can't feel my fingers.

Then I hit the ground with a thud.

Andjela screams and I hear Joe's voice above me. I hear the sound of it but I can't make out the words. And then the whack of his feet beside me sending up a shower of mud.

'What happened?' he says. 'Are you OK?'

And then I hear it above the alarm: a high-pitched howl at first, then a baying. The dogs are straining at their chains.

'*Shit!* Get up Sanda! Can you get up?'

He helps me up. Pain rips through me like a firework. Another bolt of lightning and I see the window – a black square. Did I imagine it? Joe's shouting: '*Come on!*'

We're on the fence again when there's a wrenching sound, a fierce barking and a cry, and Joe falls back to the ground rolling and clutching his leg.

One of the dogs has got loose from its leash and is snarling and jumping at him, its teeth bone white in a black mouth. I get off the fence and yell at it, wave my arms, but it doesn't move. In desperation I kick its flank. It wheels round, jaws snapping, then, it turns again, agitated. I pull Joe to his feet and we start up the fence again. I glance at Joe, see the blood washing out of him.

Then the dog comes back at us.

I can see the drool on its jowls, and behind it, something else: a pale shadow advancing. The dog seems to reel. It howls and staggers back. A burst of lightning shows a livid wound across its back that steams in the rain.

It circles and circles and is still.

Joe's ahead of me, 'Sanda!'

I have to move. I'm beyond tired and my hands are numb with cold, but I clamber up after him. Andjela's on the other side, standing back holding her shoes. She looks up, willing us on.

We get to the top, swing over and scramble down the other side. Joe hits the ground seconds before me and takes off towards the pines, holding his calf. As I jump down, I can feel the whole left side of my body tightening, the bruises knitting together so I can hardly move.

I look back through the mesh. On the other side, the carcass of the dog lies on its back, its legs limp and crooked. Someone saved us back there. Someone killed it.

The grim walls of Zbrisć bear down on us.

Who was that?

There's a commotion then from the other dog, barking and careering blindly, tearing at its leash. I hear shouting.

I look at Joe and Andjela. We run like hell, pitching headlong through wet brush. I hear an engine being started in the distance, and a thin beam of torchlight strobes the forest. But all the time in my head I can see my hand on the piece of glass, I can see the minute before I do it and I can see Mirko's blood forcing upwards through the cut.

We crash on, Andjela first, then me, then Joe. Every so often I stop for him but he waves me on.

We run for what feels like forever and I'm trying to concentrate on making my feet work until Joe calls, 'Quick, hide in here!' I turn to see him dip down and disappear. We go towards him and he pulls us into a shallow ditch where we crouch and wait. We don't speak or move. My legs are cramping and my feet are frozen. Joe's face is moon-white in the darkness.

I close my eyes and hold my breath as they pass.

After an age of waiting, we get up and head out. Andjela's up front again and I'm half looking behind me for Joe when she stops abruptly, bending at the waist and panting, her breath coming in short bursts. She can't speak but points. Below us, through the trees, is some sort of barn.

The rain is easing as we go on. The torches are far away now, receding spots of light in the dark forest. We've come down from the tree line to where the land opens out a bit. I can hear water rushing by quite close, feel a path underfoot.

What I thought was a barn is actually a one-storey house, or at least it used to be. There's no glass in the windows and the walls in places look as though they've been stoved in by a tank or with a lump hammer. The roof is just standing and there are holes in that too, where long shafts of timber poke upwards like missiles. The door's blocked so we use the nearest window and climb into one room. Bare walls, pitted and scored, and a mass of wood and concrete rubble lie in the middle of the room. At one end is the remains of a fireplace. The rain has stopped and the sky shows through the roof. A thousand stars.

We look at each other. An owl calls in the distance. My throat is dry and thick with exertion. None of us speak for a moment. And then Andjela walks to the middle of the room and starts moving the rubble, poking around underneath.

'What are you doing?' I say. In answer she straightens up and points to the fireplace. I look back at Joe who shakes his head.

'No,' he whispers, 'tell her, no fire. They'll see it.'

I translate and she nods and hangs her head, then gives me a lop-sided smile. Her throat is still blotchy but her eyes are shining.

We huddle together, cold and damp. Now and again fat drips of water from drying timbers spit and hiss on the floor. Little by little, we begin to thaw out and soon Andjela is curled up on a patch of ground and sleeping fitfully. I turn to Joe. He's sitting with his back against the wall, his hand still cradling his leg. He looks pale.

'How is it?'

'Um ... OK,' he says through his teeth.

'Let's see.'

He takes his hand away, and I can see at once it's bad. Part of his trouser leg is torn away, and there are deep teeth marks in the flesh, oozing blood.

'You need to wrap it up,' I say.

'Yeah, maybe.'

We have nothing to bind the wound except the clothes we're wearing. Without thinking, I take off my jacket and pull my T-shirt over my head.

'No! Don't do that, you'll … shit! What happened to you?'

I pull my jacket slowly back around me and I tell him about what happened and about the letter from my father.

'It was like a lifeline, you know?' I say. 'The thought that maybe after all he did care but not enough. He said – he said love was *"complicated"*. I guess he loved her too much to go against her. But now he's gone and I've got nobody.'

'Sanda. That's not true. You've got *you*. You're here. You're alive. Sanda, listen to me. *Listen!*'

He takes my arms and gently turns me towards him, his earnest face. I hold on to my sobs, choke them back. 'You're going to be OK,' he says. 'You can survive this. You will. Because, you know when it comes down to it, all any of us have is ourselves, and … and this moment. Now.'

I sniff and nod and make myself listen. Andjela stirs in her sleep behind us. He bends and whispers in my ear, warm breath: 'You've got me.'

It's so faint that afterwards I'm not sure I heard it right.

He leans back and he's quiet, and I'm starting to tear the stupid T-shirt into bandages when I see him. There's softness in his honey eyes, and all at once I know he's been watching me. I mean really *watching* me. A bird calls away in the treetops. With his eyes still on mine, he takes the T-shirt from me and puts it down. He lifts his hand and lightly brushes the tips of his fingers across my collar bone and under my bra strap. My skin prickles at his touch. He dips his hand into the hollow between my breasts, and there's a bolt, a spark from his skin into mine that makes me shudder.

'Sorry – you're cold. I ...' he says and goes to help me back on with the jacket.

I stop him and find his hand. 'No. No ... it's not that ... I ... please ... I want ...'

'Come here.'

He smiles and brings me towards him, and then I see him wince in pain. I draw back at once.

'Shit Joe. Your leg. Sorry!'

'No it's OK. It's just ... shit ... actually it's not. Sorry ...'

He falls back against the wall and lets out a long breath. I turn and grab the T-shirt. I pull off a strip that just about covers the wound but won't go all the way around his leg. I try again with another piece, but in the end, I use the whole T-shirt.

'Sanda. You shouldn't have done that,' he says.

'What? Why?'

'The T-shirt. It's freezing. You're going to freeze. Anyway, I'm OK. I'm not going to die of a dog bite am I?'

'Joe, it might have rabies.'

'Oh right. Yeah. Thanks a bunch. Rabies.'

'Sorry. I didn't mean ...'

'Sanda. It's OK.'

The stones crackle as he shifts his weight. I dig my fingernails into my palms and I wait. He reaches for my hand and presses it in his. He breathes, 'Let's try and get some sleep.'

I smile and suddenly I'm so cold. It crashes on me like a wave. I wrap my jacket tightly about me and button it. Soon his breathing is steady and I know he's sleeping. And I'm on my own.

I lie awake watching my breath coming and going in misty plumes. I can still feel his fingers on my skin, and inside me, along every artery, in every vein, my blood fizzes and whips like electricity.

13

The next thing I know, light is pouring in through windows and the thousands of little holes in the wall. My body just doesn't want to move. It's so broken from the beating that I can't lift myself up for a while. And when I do, the pain makes me gasp. An old tractor passes down the lane. The driver, a fat-faced man with hair the colour of straw, is chomping on a sandwich. I look down at Joe. My T-shirt bandage is wet with blood. He's awake though, and staring at the ground.

'How you feeling?' I say. 'Did you get any sleep?'

He shifts his weight and groans. 'Not much. I'm OK. Just hungry.'

He turns his head away from me. I force myself to talk. 'Look, we need to eat and we need to get that looked at. I think we should try to get away from here, to a village.'

'Makes sense,' he mutters. 'Are you OK?'

I nod quickly. 'I'm fine. Can you walk?'

'Of course. It's just a scratch.' He smiles. 'Look Sanda

… about last night –' I'm about to say something when he looks behind me and his eyes widen. 'Where's Andjela?'

'What?'

I turn. She's gone. He looks at me for a long time then says, 'How well d'you know her?'

'*What?*' I snap.

'All I'm saying is … can you trust her?'

I look at him. 'You –'

We're interrupted by a rustling in the weeds outside the house. We instinctively crouch into the shadows. A hand over the window ledge, and then a face: Andjela.

'Where have you been?' we both say at once.

In answer two loaves are thrown over the sill, and she climbs in after them.

'Andjela!' Joe cries, although he doesn't meet my eye, 'You're a genius! Sanda, what's the Serbian for genius?'

'I don't know,' I say, 'but you can say "*hvala*", it means "thank you".'

'*Hvala,* Andjela. Cheers!'

She's delighted, laying the loaves in front of us, like a cat bringing in a mouse. We all tear into the bread. It's delicious: fresh and yeasty, all crusty on the outside and warm and soft when I bite in. All through our feast, I try to find out where she got them. We have no money, so she must have stolen them. Maybe she isn't quite as institutionalised as I'd thought.

We rest for a bit after our meal, but when I look at Joe I know we have to get moving. He doesn't look right. He's pale, and in spite of the cold, he's sweating like he has a fever.

I think about what happened last night. I tell myself that he hadn't meant anything, he was feverish, hallucinating. I take it all – his fingertips, the pulse of electricity inside me, how he made me want him – and I ball it up and tuck it away in a corner in my head and tell myself never, ever, to go in there.

His wound needs treating properly. When, with our help, he gets to his feet, he looks even worse. Andjela disappears again and after a few minutes comes back with a large twisty stick.

I leave our little shelter with mixed feelings.

We head back into the cover of the pine forest. At one point, I hear a distant siren wailing and I wonder if it's for us. We decide to stay out of sight but to track the road. We limp through the undergrowth, Joe leaning on his stick, and Andjela helping me. With some food in me I feel better, and I'm able to think over what has happened. I still have the paper in my sock. I haven't had a chance to read it, but I don't think I want to just yet – the stakes are too high – and I'm terrified of what I'm going to find in it. The girl in the window is bothering me. She's about me – she's a part of this. I have to know. I have to go back there but I just don't know how, or when, or more importantly, how I'm going to break it to Joe.

We come out onto the road and walk alongside it for miles, all lost in our own thoughts. Now and then, a car or truck goes by, and I feel a bolt of fear. Joe's looking rougher by the minute. We've taken off the T-shirt to allow the wound to dry, and although the blood is crusting, it looks red and puffy. I look back every few minutes to see if we're being followed. I'm exhausted but I know we can't stop. I won't let us stop. Then Andjela, who's in front, turns around and points into the pines. I peer through the pines and see a curl of smoke. We turn in towards it and a little further on, a path from the road appears, winding up through the woods: two chalky tracks. We stop where the path forks and look at one another. To the left, in the distance, at the end of the track, is a house. Whitewashed, with a red tiled roof, it stands on its own, and behind it, beyond the dense trees, the white mountains loom.

'This is a mistake,' says Joe.

'I'm hungry,' I say, 'and you need help with that leg, Joe'

'Don't make me the reason,' he snaps.

I turn to Andjela. 'Andjela?'

'I think yes,' she says, and leads the way.

The first thing I notice is the smell. The sickly sweet aroma of pig shit. Right next to the house – a bit too close for comfort – is a large pen full of pigs. They're mashing about, snorting and snapping at each other. Joe and I stop to look for a moment, but Andjela goes straight up to the door and knocks. We cluster around her then and I try to look helpless. I don't have to try too hard.

The door is opened by a middle-aged woman with sagging breasts and hairy arms. She's wearing a headscarf with sketches of the Eiffel Tower on it. She folds her arms and eyes us suspiciously. Andjela and I set about pleading our case. We point to Joe's rolled-up trouser leg and the angry gash, and I give her what I hope is an eager smile. She grimaces and closes the door on us.

'Well?' says Joe.

'Wait,' I say. I can hear the woman talking inside. We wait, stamping our feet on the frozen ground to keep the cold out. After a while, the door is opened again. She gestures to us to come in. We step over the threshold with nods and 'thank you's'.

The door opens straight into a kitchen. It looks warm and homely: a large old black cooker with a chimney, a fire going, and in the middle of the room, a big table covered in a flowery plastic sheet. Every surface is covered with bits of lace, and the only things on the walls are a clock and a crucifix. I can hear the sound of a telly coming from another room.

She sits us down at the table, produces three chipped bowls and goes to the stove. My stomach is instantly on standby. Into the bowls, she ladles a lumpy stew. It smells good and it's hot and right at that moment I could've kissed her on the lips. As we eat, she sits with her red elbows on the table, and watches us. After we've eaten, she attends to Joe's leg, tutting and muttering to herself. She washes the wound in hot water, puts some kind of paste on it, and wraps his leg in a clean strip of sheeting.

Then I ask in Serbian, 'Can we use your telephone?'

She gives me a look. 'Later.'

She says we can stay until her husband comes in. She shows us into the other room and goes outside. We sit together on the floor and watch a kind of game show on the little telly. I can feel myself nodding off then Joe suddenly nudges me sharply in the ribs.

'Hey, Sanda! Something about the Scorpions ...' he whispers.

I come to and focus on the screen. The game show's over, and we're watching a lady in a purple suit reading the news. Our host is back in the room knitting fiercely.

The report is about a man's body that's been found in a car at the side of the road with a bullet in its head.

There's an image of the man, a little inset at the bottom of the screen: my father.

They say it had the look of an organised killing: Škorpioni.

There are photos of the car, parked at an angle on a lonely road at dusk, the arc lights of the police and TV crews throwing long shadows.

They know him.

The name they give him is the one from the newspaper cutting I found in the loft.

There are other pictures too, of yellowing corpses heaped on roadsides, of emaciated men staring out from behind barbed wire, of refugees tracing their way across fields with tanks and armoured cars at a sinister standstill in the background. The War.

Nothing is what it seems.

I close my eyes and I see him coming up the stairs at home in London. He looms and fades and liquefies. A heavy hand on my shoulder, the flicker of his eyes, they're all I have of him. All there was between us. A glance, a touch, the rank sweetness of garlic on his breath, all I can find to make the man I grew up with.

I realise I'm shaking. The woman mutters something I don't catch and turns back to her wool.

I feel for Joe's hand and sit very still, trying to stop my shivering. I get to my feet and ask for the toilet. The woman looks up and points out through the window.

I cross the yard to a freezing wooden shed that houses a toilet with no seat and no paper. It's plumbed straight into the ground and weeds are growing up around the bowl. I switch on the light, find a plank of wood, put it across the toilet and sit down. I take out the papers from Milanković's room. They've disintegrated in parts, but the name is still clear: *Hadžić. Senka.*

I take a deep breath and peel them apart. There are just two: the first is a certificate with the orphanage name across the top and a copy of the photograph I found in London stapled to it – the little girl.

The name on the certificate is Senka Hadžić. Written clearly on the dotted line at the bottom left-hand corner of the page is a signature. I recognise the name as the one given for my father in the cutting. It looks like his handwriting too. The paper is dated December 1995. And again my father's words come back to me: *Everything is not what you think. Nothing is what it seems.*

I find it hard to feel anything about him right now, hard to be sad, hard to forgive. And yet what he left for me, what he gave me, has at least led me this far. Like a map, or part of a map, a road back to who I am. It isn't much, but it's better than nothing. And nothing is all I thought I had.

So …

Am *I* that girl? Am I Senka Hadžić?

The other paper is a letter with the Red Cross logo at the top. There's a typewritten introduction, but the rest is written by hand in Serbian. Two things hit me: one is the name at the bottom, printed and signed, Branko Hadžić. *Branko*: the person they thought Joe was 'working' for. The person they thought had paid Joe to help me.

The second thing that leaps out at me is a copy of a colour photograph of two tiny girls, dressed in identical frilly party wear, holding hands. But what I notice at once is their eyes. They each have one green, and one blue. The names under the picture are Senka … and Sanda.

Behind them, shielding her eyes from the sun, stands a young, slim woman in a polka-dot dress. I freeze. Images flash in and out of my mind: two little girls. A man's hands around a waist. The face at the window. Joe at the orphanage saying he'd seen me. And it hits me like a steam train that the girl at Zbrisć might be the one in the first picture. And the other girl might be me.

Not Senka, but Sanda Hadžić?

But if that's the case then who's the woman in the polka dot dress? Because she looks nothing like the person I called Mum who left me back in London.

I sit there in that dank shed, my arms around my body, for about five minutes. My thoughts are interrupted by a knocking on the door.

'Sanda, are you OK in there?'

'Yeah. Yeah, I'm coming.'

I gather up the papers and stand up. Coming out of the shed, I trip over the step and the pain in my legs is unbelievable, but Joe is there as I fall, and I cling to him for a moment just to feel something real and physical instead of dread and confusion and excitement all mixed into one. He pulls me into him.

Then, 'Your dad ... shit, Sanda, I'm sorry.'

'I know,' I say, 'but I ... I ... well, Joe look at this.'

I bring him into the light of the toilet shed and show him.

'Branko!' he breathes. 'Shit. But I don't get it ... So this girl, this *is* you? *You're* Senka?'

I shake my head. 'I don't think so. Look.' I point to the names under the photo: *Senka* and *Sanda*.

He peers at it, then looks back at me. 'Twins. The eyes.'

'I know. That has to be me, yeah?'

'Then that girl at the orphanage. The one I thought was you ...'

'I saw her. I know I did, last night. At a window, when we were climbing the fence. I saw her.'

'And the letter from Branko. What does it say?'

'He's looking for his daughters.'

'Christ. So it could be ... Branko's what? Your *dad*?'

I bite my lip. 'Joe, I have to ...'

'What?'

'I have to get her out.'

'No – Sanda, we'll just go to the police and tell them,

and when we get home we can –'

'Home? I don't *have* a home. I have nowhere to go. I have no relatives in England. Not one. Nobody's going to be looking for me. This is it. She *is* my family. My sister. And she's been stuck in that place all her life. I have to.'

'Right.'

'What?'

'I'm thinking,' he says, then after a moment, 'let's get back inside.'

He lopes off towards the house on his bad leg, and I wonder how it's doing. He seems a little better. But he's distracted. I follow slowly and I'm way away from all of this. I'm a million miles away, rattling about the earth like a mad satellite.

Back inside, Andjela and the woman are back in the little room talking. Andjela is sitting at her feet helping her to wind wool. They look up when we come in. There are noises coming from upstairs: someone in heavy boots moving about on bare boards, then a creaking on the stairs.

Into the room comes a burly man dressed in a cardigan and trousers that look way too small for him. The material is stretched so tight across his buttocks that I can see his checked underpants peeping through. His teeth stick out like a little yellow shelf. He stares at us all and then grunts at his wife to join him in the kitchen.

I can't really say why but I don't like the look of him and I'm seriously beginning to think we were crazy to come here.

I whisper to Joe, 'They're going to hand us over, Joe. I know they are. I can see it in his face. That's what they're talking about.'

'He's all right,' he says. 'He's just a farmer. Anyway, he's the best we've got right now.'

But still I feel anxious. We're trapped in the little room. There's no back door that I can see. The only way out leads through the kitchen. I pinch back the net curtains. The windows are far too small even for Andjela to crawl through.

'Shit.'

Boots on the flagstones. He's coming back.

He says in English, 'You are lost? Yes? You are English?'

Joe nods, 'We ... yes, we're lost. Can we use your telephone?'

He ignores the bit about the telephone. 'You on *holiday*?' he says looking at Andjela with narrow eyes.

He hoots with laughter then and when he throws his head back I can actually see the undersides of his teeth.

'Er ... No,' says Joe. 'We just need to use your phone to ...'

The man raises a hand to cut him off, then turns to me, 'And who are you?'

'I'm Sanda. We just need ...'

'Sanda is Bosnian name. You is Bosnian? Not English?'

'I grew up in England. My parents are from Serbia.'

He screws up his eyes and studies me. 'Your father and your mother Serbian?'

'Yes.'

'OK. Truth. Where have you come from?' he says.

I look at Joe and take a breath. 'The orphanage on the mountain. Zbrisć.'

His wife claps a hand across her mouth.

'Madame Milanković?' he asks.

My palms prickle with sweat. Joe's eyes are wide.

'You *know* her?' I ask.

'Of course,' he nods briskly, 'everybody knows.'

Joe says quickly, 'I think we should be going. The police will be looking for us. Come on Andjela.'

I don't know whether or not she catches the panic in his voice but she gets to her feet and moves towards the door.

'You stay,' says the man, 'I telephone for you.'

Joe is standing by the door to the kitchen; he jerks his head in the direction of the front door: 'Let's go.'

He grabs me by the hand and starts to make for the door. Andjela slips past too, but I can see at once it's not her they want. Joe's pulling me on but something's stopping me.

I can't go.

I have to finish this, to see it through and I know it's stupid but I tug my hand free and shake my head. Andjela's already outside.

Joe looks at me in confusion, *'Sanda, come on!'*

'Joe, just go! Go and get help! Please!'

We're in the kitchen. He's caught for a moment in the front doorway. The man grabs at his clothes but Joe's too strong. He throws him off and aims a punch at him. The man staggers back nursing his jaw.

'*Sanda!*'

'No,' I say evenly. 'I have to go back. This is my fight.'

I know I'm hurting him; I can only hope he'll understand. Then he's gone.

From the kitchen window, I watch them stumble across the farmyard, Joe leaning on Andjela.

They make it to the lane and disappear into the undergrowth. I knit my arms tight across my chest.

I will not cry.

14

The man goes back into the little room. I hear him cursing to himself, then a muffled phone conversation while the woman stares at me like I'm something she's found under a drain cover. When he comes back into the kitchen, he doesn't look happy.

'Sit down!'

I sit at the table. I say in Serbian, 'It's OK. I'll go back. I know you called them.'

For the longest time he stares at me, then he says something to his wife and she goes to the sink. To the sounds of clatter and running water, he sits down on a little wicker chair by the fire in the range that creaks under his weight. He puts his hands on his knees and leans back and sighs.

'Your friends are very bad,' he says in Serbian now, 'very bad. If she catches them she'll send them to the House.'

'The *house*? What house?'

He scratches his thighs and the fabric squeaks and winces under his fingers.

'The House: a place where bad children go to learn to obey; children who can't behave, children like you who run away.'

'You mean Zbrisć?'

He shakes his head: 'Another place. In the woods.'

'So –'

He stops me. 'No more,' he says. 'Tell me what you were doing at Zbrisć.'

'I was taken,' I say, 'by force. Taken from my home in England.'

I tell him what I know and what I think I know. He listens carefully and picks at his eyebrows.

'War is difficult,' he says.

'War? What d'you mean? This isn't about the War.'

He shrugs. 'Everything is about the War.'

He falls silent and we both gaze into the fire. His wife quietly leaves the room.

After a while, I pull out the damp pages from my pocket and hand them to him.

'I think that's me.' I lean across and indicate. 'I think that's me and my … my twin. My sister. I think she's at Zbrisć and I want to find out why.'

And my mind takes me back to Andjela's drawing on the wall. She was trying to show me my sister.

He turns the papers over in his hands.

He bends to stoke up the dwindling fire and I see the top of a tattoo on his neck – two black pincers curling upwards towards his left ear. They remind me of the crab tattoo I saw on one of my abductors. Then I realise with horror that it isn't a crab, it's a scorpion. And in the same moment I recall the scar on my father's neck. He always said it was a dog bite. Could that have been the remains of a tattoo that was removed?

He sees me looking. 'Škorpioni,' he smiles. 'Yes. We don't like trouble.'

Without a word, he crumples the pages into a ball and throws them onto the fire. I stare in disbelief as they burn down to tiny ashes and rise like black butterflies up the chimney. The photograph blackens and shrinks in the embers.

'What are you doing?' I shout. 'What?! *Why?*'

He looks at me, flicks his tongue over his teeth, gets to his feet and says, 'It's best for you to go back to Zbrisć. No more questions. Do as you are told.'

He gets up, goes into the other room and closes the door behind him. There's something in his manner that I can't place. Sure, he's brusque and dismissive but there's more. I think he's frightened of something.

I hear them talking in urgent voices. The door opens and it's his wife. In trembling hands she holds a shotgun. I hear him on the phone in the background.

I try to smile at her – I don't want her pulling the trigger by accident – but I find all I can manage is an odd kind of leer. He comes back into the kitchen and takes up the gun.

He says, 'They're coming for you. Madame Milanković. She's a good lady. She'll look after you very well. You will be safe there. No police.'

They do come for me of course. A battered Fiat sputters up the lane and we go out to meet it. I know it from the orphanage. Milanković is driving, and two women I haven't seen before are seated in the back, arms folded, looking stern. Before Milanković even gets out she's bellowing at the man. She's not talking about me this time, but about Joe and Andjela. He nods, goes back into the house and returns, shotgun in hand. I know that soon after we leave, he'll be hunting them on her orders. I pray that they've had enough of a head start.

He hands me over with a warning look. I go meekly enough and squeeze into the back of the Fiat on the torn seats, between my guards. I try to tell myself that Joe and Andjela are well on their way by now, probably at a police station telling them where I am.

As for me, at least I now know what I want. I want to find Senka. My father, or the man who called himself my father, is dead. Another thread has been cut. And my mother? Were they both lying to me? I want to know my story. I want to know where I fit.

Milanković is very tight-lipped on the way and as I can look neither left nor right because of the women on either side of me, I spend the journey staring at the back of her neck. It's greasy and pitted with scars, and there are fine ridges of grime where it hasn't been washed. The smell in the little car is pretty rank all over and it can't just be my companions – I try to remember the last time *I* had a proper wash, in hot water with soap.

It's weird how quickly we get back. It seemed so long

on foot. I sleep in a locked room that night. And as I sleep, I dream again of hands holding me, gripping me tightly, but this time we're moving. Someone's driving me away from where I want to be, and the hands are holding on to stop me falling or running away. I'm on the back of some kind of open truck. I see canvas flapping, the woods and the glittering road, and hear the creak of the boards. I wake up shouting.

In the morning, I wait in the room. I walk up and down, occasionally stopping to bang on the door and call out for someone. Nothing. Judging by what sun I can see from the window, it's mid-afternoon before I hear the heavy door being unlocked. The two women from the car march me down to Madame Milanković's office and stand me outside while they knock. I wonder if they're new. One of the women is skinny with a wheezy chest and the other looks like she's trying to grow a beard. They both look nervous. But me – it's odd because I'm not scared any more, I'm furious. I want answers and I want to see the girl I think is my sister. In fact, I don't think I feel afraid of anything or anyone any more.

Waiting outside that room, I feel like the fucking Terminator.

But inside, I don't have the showdown I've just seen unfolding in my head, the one where I thump the table and demand my sister be brought in. And that's because, sitting in a low armchair in the corner of the room, is my mother.

She's wearing a thin grey turtle-neck jumper, tight jeans and rubber boots. Her hair is tied in a loose pony tail. She's lost weight and the bones in her face are sharper than ever.

'Mum?' the word hurts.

She gets up, awkwardly somehow, her arms hanging at her sides. Her face is hard. She moves across to the window and hooks a wisp of hair back over her ear.

Milanković is hunched in her desk chair, smoking. She has a strange smile on her face. 'Yes. Your mother is here,' she says.

'Mum, what have you ...? Why did you ...?' I'm crying now but she turns and looks out of the window. 'Mum?'

Milanković sits up, blinks like a toad. 'Your mother has come to take you.'

'I'm not going anywhere without Senka.'

'No. You will go. It's arranged. It's time.'

'I want my sister! Get me my sister!'

My mother speaks, her face still averted. 'She's not here.'

'Then *where* is she?'

Then she turns and looks at me. Her lips tighten against her gums.

'You never stop,' she says. 'I am sick of you. Always asking questions. You want to see this girl? *You want to see her?* Don't worry. You'll see her. And you'll see what she is. She's a pig. Dirty and stupid, like all of you.'

I stare at her. 'All of who?'

She waves a hand at me and glances at Milanković.

I say again, *'All of who?'*

I'm shouting now. I'm aware of the door opening behind me but Milanković bats away whoever it is. An image looms up at me from the past, hazy then clear: *those hands around my waist.* I'm finding it hard to get my breath.

My mother walks back to the chair, perches on the arm. She crosses her legs and inspects her fingernails. Milanković gets up and offers her a cigarette. She takes it and lights it slowly.

I breathe, 'You lied to me. All my life you lied.'

She says nothing, only draws on the cigarette, squinting as the smoke balloons about her. I swallow hard. Milanković comes towards me but I'm too quick for her. I bolt from the room and into the hall. *'Senka! Senka! Where are you?'*

I tear along the corridor and into the quad outside where I scan the windows at the back and call again: *'Senka!'* No reply. I'm about to go back inside but my tiredness and racking pain get the better of me and I sink down on the kitchen step and put my head in my hands.

Then I hear Milanković's voice up close: 'We told you she's not here.'

'No!'

I'm still screaming and kicking as the two women manhandle me through the building and into the back of a waiting car. They have a last conversation and a brief, cold embrace holding their faces away from each other, and then my mother gets in the driving seat and the bearded lady gets in next to me.

'Let me go!'

My mother says nothing. I reach over the back of her seat to grab at her hair but the woman holds my hands in an iron grip.

My mother, sitting upright at the wheel, turns the car down the drive. I'm a prisoner again. All I can hope is that Joe and Andjela are safe.

I say, 'Where are we going?' No answer. *'Where are we going?'*

The car lurches and jolts over pits in the road. I try again: 'You know what they did to me? Back in London? Back in the house? They drugged me and threw me in the back of a truck. Did you ask them to do that? Did you want them to do that to me? I don't understand. My friend Joe was −'

She glances in the rear-view mirror: 'They thought the boy was −'

'Working for someone looking for me.'

'Looking for you,' she says. 'Yes.'

'For Branko, for my father, my real father − the man who's looking for his daughters.'

Her face stiffens at the mention of him. 'Yes. Your *real* father.'

'I *know* he's looking for us.'

She slows the car to a halt and twists round, her elbow in my face. 'You think you know everything, don't you? You think he *cares*?' It's like a punch in the head. 'About *you*? About the other one? He doesn't care about you. It's not *you* he's looking for, it's *me*.'

I feel sick. My throat is dry. I can't swallow.

She thrusts the car into gear and takes a turn, which takes us up into the mountains. There's salt in my eyes and throat, and a pinching in my chest.

I say quietly, *'Please?'*

She ignores me and shifts in her seat as she looks ahead. 'You're just like him. Selfish.'

'You're lying,' I say. 'He's not … he wouldn't …'

'You wait and see.'

'Just tell me!'

'You shut up! You shut up your stupid mouth or I hit you! *Shut up!*'

It's then that I realise I hate this woman I called my mother.

And I begin to wonder what *she* did in the War.

15

With the sun sinking behind us, we go down country lanes, along freezing, rutted tracks, always going up. We pass farmhouses, strange and square, with tall pyramid roofs, now and then, we see a solitary white stone church.

We follow a road along a wide river to a cobbled bridge. At either end of the bridge stands a tiny church, wedding-cake white with little arched doors. As we cross the river, we see lights, and a small village comes into view. A few crooked stone houses with red roofs, a well with a fountain in the square, and an inn with a black slate roof and a high wrought iron balcony jutting like a lip over the river. The inn is called брод, which means The Ship.

My mother parks the Fiat and pokes Beardie awake. She gets out and locks the doors, brings out her phone and dials. I watch her going into the inn, snapping angrily into her phone. Beardie and I eye each other warily.

Minutes later she comes out, rubbing her arms. 'We'll stop here to eat.'

Inside the inn, it's low and gloomy but there's a fire burning in the hearth and a smell of wood smoke and roasting onions. Mum has to stoop to go in through the door, straightens at once and gets out her phone again. We all go to the chairs by the fire. I lean in and the heat licks around me.

The bartender seems nice. He's a tall man with a ginger beard, and he wears a striped apron round his waist. He brings us each a bowl of steaming meat stew and a hunk of bread. I could refuse it to make a point but I'm so hungry and so cold, I decide to give myself a break. As he puts the stew in front of me, I accidentally knock the bread onto the floor. He crouches down next to me, picks it up and stuffs it in his pocket. He pushes himself up and goes to the kitchen. In a minute he's back kneeling beside me again with a bigger piece of bread. He places it in my lap and smiles. It's crusty on the outside, freckled with flour, and as I tear it apart the warmth of it sends a yeasty tingle springing into my nose and mouth. He watches me eat and in that moment something passes between us and I know this man has a heart.

I watch my mother eating. Not for the first time I wonder how she lost her teeth. I finish in no time and he's there with a second bowl and more bread for me. My mother goes outside again, pacing up and down, talking on her phone. I see her come and go past the window. She seems angry and agitated.

I smile at the innkeeper and he smiles back.

Over the fireplace, is a mirror. I haven't seen my

reflection in days. It's like looking at another person. My face is thinner and I can see the bones of my skull. My skin is dry as paper, and my hair is frosted with dirt.

Stay alive, Sanda. Stay alive.

I'm coming back from the bathroom a bit later, when from a shadowy corner I hear, 'Hey.'

It's the innkeeper, his bulky form pressed against the wall of the passageway. My mother's back inside now; I can hear her barking into her phone about 'arrangements' to be made.

I step towards him. 'What is it?' I ask in Serbian.

'Are you *OK*?' he says in a throaty whisper.

'I … I'm …' It's hard to know where to begin.

'You seem …' He hesitates. 'Stop me if I'm interfering, but I thought you … who's that you're with?'

'Um … your accent?' I say. 'You're not Serbian? Do you speak English?' He smiles. I say, 'I'm from England. That's my mother I'm with, or at least …' I stop and swallow, 'I mean I speak Serbian but my English is better …'

'Me too,' he says, in English now, 'I *am* English. I'm Peter. This is my place.'

'I'm Sanda. How come you're here?'

'I was here with the United Nations after the war and I liked it. I married a Serbian girl and I settled here. Beats Nottingham any day. And you?'

I have a second to make up my mind, and I decide I'm going to trust him. I'm going to ask for his help.

'I – what I tell you, you probably won't believe but it's true. I swear on my life it's all true.'

I tell him everything. There in the dark, rough little passageway with its stone floor and smell of spilled beer. He nods and murmurs as I hurry and stumble over events and times. When I'm finished, he says: 'Nothing would surprise me after that war. Nothing. So, you think this Branko might be your father?'

'I think so. I hope so. I want ...'

'And her? Who's she then?' He jerks his chin in the direction of the bar. And it dawns on me that I have absolutely no idea. I'm about to speak but he says, 'It's just that she −'

'The Škorpioni ...' I break in. 'Have you heard of them?' I tell him about my father, at least the man I thought was my father. He scratches his beard thoughtfully.

'God, yes. The Škorpioni are a really powerful organisation. A lot of police are in their pockets. They started up in the War as a paramilitary group fighting the Bosnians but they're much bigger than that now. They've got politicians, police, businesses, international contacts, fingers in lots of pies. They're a kind of ... a kind of Mafia I suppose. You fall foul of them and you're really in trouble.'

'I wonder if she's involved in some way ...'

'Yes,' he says, looking down the passage. 'Yes. I think she might be. Where's she taking you?'

'I have no idea.'

He nods. He seems distant. He's looking over at my mother who's still deep in conversation on the phone.

'You better get back. You'll be missed. Let me have a think.'

I return to my place by the fire, and Mum steps away from the bar and carries on her phone call out of earshot. Beardie stares vacantly into the flames as they drive cinder and sparks upwards into the black.

I think about my sister.

She's in my head now. I can feel her moving, breathing, lacing her fingers, her tongue against her teeth, her eyes opening and closing, and the thread and the web between us, strong as rope.

My mother pays the bill with coins counted one by one onto the bar counter. I catch Peter's eye as he collects them. She ushers us out and into the car, gets in and turns the ignition. It doesn't start. She tries again, and the engine coughs and belches and dies with a whirring sound. Peter's watching from the door, and he winks at me as he comes over.

'What's the trouble?' he asks, folding his arms across his chest.

'I don't know,' she snaps. 'It was fine before. Do you know anything about cars?'

'A bit,' he says. 'Why don't you go and have a sit down inside while I take a look?'

The car shifts as she gets out, and he reaches inside to open the bonnet.

'Could the young one give me a hand?' he calls.

She looks at me and says, 'I'll be watching.'

'Get under here,' he says from beneath the bonnet. I join him as he pinches cables and taps the battery.

'I don't know anything about cars I'm afraid,' I say.

'I do. That's how I broke it.'

'Sorry?'

'Wanted to buy you a bit of time.'

'Thank you.'

'I've called someone.'

'Who?'

'For her,' he says. I straighten up and look at him. He says, 'You don't know do you?'

'Know what?'

'Your mum is Kristina Perška.'

And yet again, the map in my head is torn up and thrown into the air.

'Who?'

'You don't know the name?'

I shake my head. My breath is coming in shallow rasps. I'm hot and cold waiting for what's coming.

'I thought I recognised her – I Googled her picture just to be sure. She's wanted for war crimes. She helped run an asylum, well, that's what they called it. It was basically a concentration camp. Thousands of non-Serbs were put there in the early nineties – people were beaten, raped, starved, left to rot.'

I'm struggling to stay standing, to breathe, to be inside my body just now. I have to repeat what he's said to me, in my head, over and over like a broken record.

He rubs my back. 'Are you OK?'

'I … I … don't know. She … a *concentration camp*?' The pictures from the news in the farmhouse come back to me. Piles of bodies, people displaced and starving.

Barbed wire. Barbed wire fences. And my mother, her eyebrows knitted, gluing broken gnomes at a kitchen table in north London.

'Sanda – I'm sorry.'

'I ... I ...what did she do?'

'She was one of the people running the thing – directing operations. She was notorious. They called her The Butcher.'

16

A blackness, chill and creeping, folds me into it, muffles me, and I close my eyes against it and try to breathe.

'I know. I'm sorry,' he says. 'She's wanted for war crimes. There's a huge reward for her capture. I called some people I know. They'll bring her in. The local police can't always be trusted.'

'*Wanted?*'

'Maybe that's why they came back here. Maybe the police in the UK are on to them. They had to get out. They'll have lots of friends here, a place to hide, and, like I say, the local cops will turn a blind eye. Some people still either sympathise with the Škorpioni or are so scared of them, they won't come forward.'

'But why take me? Why not leave me at Zbrisč?'

He scratches his chin. 'I don't know. I don't know why *you're* here. Seems weird for someone like her to have taken a baby in the first place.'

My spine is cold water.

'I don't think that is true. I think he does want to find you. I think he's been looking for a long time.'

'He could be anywhere,' I say. The words slip out of me: 'He could be dead.'

Silence and then Peter speaks quickly. 'No. I don't think so. Listen, I'll do some digging; see if we can't stir something up. He may have left a forwarding address through the Red Cross. They've got a missing persons website. Just have a bit of faith, Sanda.'

I smile but I'm empty. 'I think I lost it.'

I feel awkward all of a sudden. I twist the sleeve of my top around my thumb and swing my feet onto the floor. I bend to put on my boots, for something to do.

Peter says, 'We'll do all we can. Natalija can find out if your sister's in this place, and I can make some enquiries about Branko.'

I'm an upturned boat, splintered and drifting.

I say, 'Thank you.' In my head, I hear the echo: *'Thank you.'*

Natalija gets up and goes to the door. 'You'll come down and eat with us?'

I smile, nod. Peter turns to follow her.

I call after him, 'What if Kristina's right? What if he doesn't want me … us?'

'Don't listen to her.'

'OK, but what if he has another family now? If that letter was written a long time ago? If he's forgotten about …'

'Don't be daft. Yes, he may have another family but

that doesn't mean he won't want you.'

At that moment, I feel more alone than ever. Actually *alone* isn't right – I think I mean *lonely*. I nod miserably.

Then, I don't know why but I blurt out: 'Do you have children?'

There's a pause. 'No. No we don't. Natalija miscarried, and it was bad. We can't have any more.'

'Oh God. I'm sorry. I didn't mean to ...'

'It's OK. It's OK. Let's go down.'

I go downstairs and in spite of everything, I manage to have a good evening. They ask me all about my life at home, about my school, my friends, about Joe. It turns out Peter knows north London well, and talking about it kind of grounds me a bit, makes it feel real. Like something about me is true. And all the time I can't help but think how it would feel to be their daughter.

I dream about Joe: we're back at Zbrisć. Except it isn't Zbrisć, it's school, and in the classrooms are wild-eyed children with shaven heads and toothless mouths. And all around, as ever, the black pines crowd in, right up to the windows, through the windows, their feathery fingers reaching for me.

17

In the morning, I wake up feeling a bit better about stuff. I look at myself in the mirror and my skin and hair seem a little softer.

Later, when Natalija's at work, Peter takes me into the nearest town in their pick-up truck, and stands around awkwardly in the only teen clothes shop, with Iron Maiden on the PA, while I pick out a few clothes. Natalija came to me last night and pressed some money into my hand.

'After all you've been through, you should do something normal – go and buy some clothes – something for your hair.'

Obviously she's told Peter to take me, and I can see how uncomfortable it makes him. In the end, I say would he like to do his own shopping and I'll meet him by the truck. He's so pleased to get away, he practically runs out of the shop, almost knocking a mannequin into a group of girls who give him a look.

The selection isn't great but I choose a couple of pairs

of shorts, some coloured tights, a stripy jumper, a hoodie, a large army-style jacket, some warm gloves and a cool beanie hat to cover my hair.

I leave my old clothes in the shop, and I'm wandering back to where the truck is parked when I see Peter hurrying towards me. He's sweating and he looks anxious.

'Hi Peter. What's up?'

'Get in! Get in the truck!'

'What is it?'

He opens the door and bundles me in, then gets into the driver's side and guns the engine. 'I just had a call from Natalija.'

'And?'

'Well, you know she's been asking around in other hospitals?'

'Senka! She's found her?'

He shakes his head. 'No trace of her. But that's not it. Natalija has a friend, Yana, who works in a hospital in Belgrade. Yana just called to say a boy was brought in late last night.'

My heart somersaults in my chest.

'Oh God. Joe?'

'They're not sure but Yana thinks it's him. The description you gave –'

'Joe.'

'You mustn't get your hopes up. It may not be him at all. Was there anything else about him?'

I think. 'He had a bite, a bad dog bite on his leg.'

'That fits. This boy had a bad laceration. We need to

He goes on, 'I hope your friends are OK but they're going to be running for their lives. You all need to be very careful who you trust.'

'She's going to kill me, isn't she? That's why she's taking me.'

He looks at me and then quickly away. 'I don't know, Sanda,' he says. 'I don't know.'

Before I have time to say anything, we hear the sound of a car roaring up the track. I squat down with Peter and watch as a black Land Rover appears. A thick set man in a bullet proof jacket almost falls out of the car and crouches behind it, a gun in his hand.

'That's him,' says Peter in a low voice. 'I called him. He'll bring her in. He'll see justice done; can't trust the police. They wouldn't touch her. They've got too much to lose.'

I feel strangely distanced from the scene as though that's what it really is — just a scene from a TV drama. The man runs towards the inn and backs against the wall. He twists on his heel, gun raised, and slides around the door frame. We hear a door slamming inside and seconds later, an engine being violently revved.

Suddenly, a battered Volvo wheels past us from the back of the inn.

'Shit! She's taken my car!' says Peter.

The gunman bursts out of the inn and fires. The bullet screams into the back of the car, shattering the rear window.

She's gone, Beardie with her. He barrels back into the Land Rover and gives chase. Balloons of dust obscure them. Another shot smacks in the distance and I hear a squeal of brakes.

'Are you OK?' Peter says, looking at me with concern.

'Are you sure it's her? That she's this Perška person? Are you sure?'

'Sanda, come with me.'

In a daze, I follow him into the inn.

Inside, I sink into a chair. I'm dimly aware of him behind the bar talking on the phone.

'Sanda? Sanda?' He's off the phone. 'Sanda. That was my wife.'

'Oh.' I pull myself back down to earth.

'She's a doctor. I've asked her to make enquiries about your friends. About your sister. We're going to have to be careful. Like I say, the Škorpioni have a great deal of power. In the most unexpected places.'

'Yes … yes …'

'Are you OK?'

'Er …Yes. I'm just a bit dazed I suppose.'

'Look. I think you should stay with us tonight. You can't do anything right now. Why don't you try and get some sleep? I'll wake you if I hear anything.'

I sleep like a baby. I sleep for all the time I've spent dirty and cold and hungry and afraid; and in my dreams the hands around my waist shift and buckle, loosen their grip. I lift my eyes away from them and look out at what I'm leaving behind: a woman screaming. And then nothing: a hole in my head, in my memory. And then all around, mountains and pine forests pressing in on me, hemming me in. I feel my London life slipping further and further out of sight. Lauren. School. Everything.

A knocking wakes me up. It's dark. I've been asleep all day but the moment I open my eyes I think of Joe. And I know something's wrong.

'Sanda?'

A voice on the other side of the door.

'Mmm?'

The door opens and Peter's there. Behind him, a woman as tall as him, with dark hair and green eyes. She's smiling.

She comes towards me, says in English, 'Hi.'

She has a soft, husky voice and she smells of rosemary. I sit up and wriggle back against the bed head.

'Hi. I'm Sanda.'

She laughs, and looks back at him. 'I know. I'm Natalija,' she says. 'And you know Peter.'

She sits next to me on the bed, takes my head in her hands and moves it gently from side to side, looking at me intently. I'm suddenly horribly conscious of my hedgehog hair and blotchy skin under her touch. 'Are you all right? You've had a lot to take in.'

I shake my head. 'I'm worried about my friends,' I say, and to Peter, 'What about the guy with the gun, did he catch her?'

He shakes his head. 'Not this time.'

Natalija looks over at Peter and then back at me.

'We must hope your friends can get away.'

And Peter says, 'No news is good news,' but my chest

tightens all the same.

Natalija says, 'Tell me about your sister.'

OK. Weird to be asked that. Weird to think about having a sister – in the normal way of: *where does your sister go to school?* Or, *I like your sister's shoes.*

'Um … she … well it's funny because I don't know anything about her. I've never met her. But I think we're identical. We have the same eyes …'

'They're beautiful,' she says.

'Er … thanks.'

'Peter told me your story. I want to help. I think they might have taken her to a kind of hospital. Some of the older children go there from Zbrisć. Not good. It's very important we try to get to her as soon as possible. But –'

'A hospital?'

She looks at Peter. 'A kind of hospital. For …'

Peter says, 'An asylum.'

My sister. 'Why?'

'Somewhere to keep her quiet,' says Peter. 'They don't pull their punches these people. Deaths are difficult. People ask questions, but in there, you can keep a person in these places forever.'

I draw my knees up tight and hook my fingers around them.

Under my breath I say, 'It doesn't make sense. None of this. Why they wanted me here, why they've taken her. Mum – Kristina – she said my real father wasn't even looking for *us.* She said it was her he wanted.'

Natalija closes her hand over mine.

'Andjela? Was there a girl with him? What about her?'

'I asked but they didn't know anything about a girl. I hope she's OK.' To Peter she says, 'Yana says you can stay the night in her flat.'

I sit in silence thinking of Andjela alone in the forest, maybe hurt, certainly hungry.

I catch a look between them.

Peter goes to her and says, 'You'll be OK here?'

Natalija smiles at him – a loving smile, and I think of my parents – my fake parents. They never smiled at each other that way.

'You can take my car.'

I sleep on the journey and wake with a headache and a dry mouth as we slow with the traffic into the country's capital. It feels strange to be in a city again. Wet streets shine in the headlights, castle walls, old stone, church domes and glassy skyscrapers lean in on us.

Yana, I learn, is a doctor. Her flat is on the fourth floor of a high block.

She greets us at the door: a delicate, bright-eyed woman, with thick chestnut hair piled into a messy bun and glasses pinching at the end of her nose. The flat is small and cramped but comfortable and it smells of polish. It looks out onto a concrete square where there's a giant statue of an elephant.

Peter hails a taxi and we go with Yana to the hospital.

When we get there, Yana takes charge. We're directed up to the 5th floor and cover what seems like miles of squeaking linoleum along windowless corridors under the glare of strip lights. The reek of disinfectant is overpowering. At last, she points to distant double doors.

She says, 'That's it.'

I want to run, but I can't. At that moment I think all I feel is fear – I'm actually frightened of seeing him again. After all I've put him through, will he really want to see *me*? I let Yana and Peter walk on ahead while I hang back. When we get to the ward, I know straight away something isn't right. The doors seem to be locked and there's a notice taped to the glass with 'KONTAMINOVAN!' written in pen.

Yana buzzes but no one comes. There's paper covering the inside of the glass doors so we can't see through.

She buzzes again.

After a while, there is muttering and whispering and then the click-clack of heels. The door opens, and a young nurse in scrubs is standing there. In the background, I see two men talking in whispers. Yana asks about Joe.

The nurse looks at us and shakes her head.

Yana says, 'I need to speak to the doctor.'

In answer, the nurse shuts the door, but after a few moments, it's opened by a man with tired eyes and a grey goatee. He's wearing a grubby white coat over a dark suit. He stands back to let us in. I see at once that the ward is empty.

The conversation takes all of sixty seconds. Yana speaks in an urgent whisper and the doctor says very little. He looks at the floor, arms folded, and every so often, his eyelids lift, creasing the skin at his temples. The room is ice cold but I notice he's sweating.

Then I see why. At a desk in the corner of the room, the young nurse is watching us closely and after a moment, she picks up the phone. There's a faint click as she does so. At once the man straightens, offers a tentative hand to Yana and makes his excuses. He walks away smartly and his heels ring on the linoleum. The nurse watches him go, the receiver to her ear.

Yana pushes us out fast. 'I don't trust them,' she says. 'We need to hurry.'

'Where's Joe? Is he OK?'

'They said … they said when he came round he seemed disturbed, violent. They had to sedate him. He's been moved.'

'Moved?'

She flashes a look at Peter. 'He's in a secure hospital now.'

'You mean like a prison?' I say.

'I mean like a hospital for —' she begins.

Peter says, 'It's a … it's a kind of asylum.'

I think of Senka and what Natalija said about what might have happened to her. I stare at my shoes: the laces are looped over either side, coarse and fraying and speckled with rain. I'm breathing.

Peter goes on: 'We'll get him out. Yana's a match for any old scorpion.'

He doesn't sound convinced. The clock on the wall says quarter to midnight.

'We can't do more tonight,' he says. 'We'll go there in the morning.'

Late into the night as I doze on Yana's sofa, they sit and drink and smoke, and talk about how to get into, and out of the asylum. It's dawn when Peter's phone rings. He takes it in the other room and comes back after two minutes, smiling.

'Well. Whaddya know?'

'What?'

'That was Natalija.'

'And?'

'She's had a visitor.'

My heart leaps and he nods. 'Mr Hadžić. He came looking for you.'

'Oh! Where is he now?'

'Hotel.'

'And he's coming back?'

'Of course he's coming back. If all goes well with Joe, we'll be back this evening.'

I see Yana give him a pointed glance that I know I'm not supposed to see. I know it's to do with Joe. She puts out her cigarette and goes into the kitchen.

The asylum doesn't look as I imagined it would. It looks like a kind of cottage hospital, with ivy on the walls and a few expensive cars parked at angles in the drive. Peter and I wait in the car while Yana goes in.

She returns about five minutes later and pokes her head in through the window. 'OK. He's in there. We don't have long.'

Peter looks behind her. 'That was quick. How do you know?'

'Because they said he wasn't. I'd hardly said good morning before they said he wasn't there and I knew they were lying. That nurse must have called them, warned them. And … they know I know.'

She shoots a look at Peter. He says, 'I should have gone.'

'What do you mean?'

'Too risky for you – as a doctor and –'

'I'm a person first.'

'Yeah, but –'

I open the door. 'I'm going to get him!' I say.

Yana pushes me back and slams the door. Her face is white and her eyes glitter.

'Not you! Get back in the car! You go, and you'll end up in there too! And you'll both end up dead! Have you understood *anything* you've been told about these people? Stay out of sight and let us handle this!' She softens her voice and adds, *'Please?'*

I do as I'm told. I wait, crouched under a scratchy rug, for what seems like hours listening to the sound of my own breathing, until I hear them coming. I throw the rug off and sit up. I see Yana first, marching purposefully towards the car. After her comes Peter, backing down the steps, talking to a white-coated woman in rapid Serbian. He's half carrying, half supporting what looks at first like a heavy roll of carpet. It's Joe. He's dressed in nothing but a hospital gown and is wrapped in a thick blanket. His legs don't seem to work and his eyes roll white in his head.

Peter manoeuvres him against the car, and I open the door and shuffle across to make room. Yana already has the engine running as we pull Joe's limp form inside. As she reverses the car, the woman comes running down the steps holding a phone. She runs at the car as if to try and stop us. Too late. Yana yanks the wheel, swerves around her and bombs through the open gates onto the road. As we pass the woman on the drive, she looks straight at me.

Yana revs the engine and we race back to the flat through the morning traffic. Next to me, Joe is mumbling incoherently, his head lolling against the seat. His face is scratched and bruised.

'What's the matter with him?' I say. 'What have they done? Is this the accident?'

Yana looks back over her shoulder as we slow in the traffic. 'It's probably Thorazine – it's a heavy sedative. It'll wear off in a few hours I hope. Natalija can check him out properly when you get back.'

Peter, who's been very quiet, says softly, 'I think we're being followed.'

'I know,' she says.

I twist in my seat and see a large black estate car tailing us.

Yana says in alarm, 'Get down Sanda! Stay out of sight!' She weaves the car in and out of traffic and I'm thrown against Joe and then back against the window. 'Shit, I can't shake him!'

'Stay calm,' Peter says. 'The boy –'

'Peter! He has a gun! Jesus!'

'Turn there! There!'

There are shouts and the sound of horns from the street and I'm thinking what I've done to these people by coming into their lives, what danger they've put themselves in by helping me.

'Missed it! Fuck!'

'Next turn. There. Stay calm.'

'I'm not calm, I'm fucking scared.'

We speed up. And I hear a sigh from Yana as she leaves the tail behind.

Peter puts a hand on her arm. 'He's gone. You did it.'

I find myself reaching for Joe's hand and gripping it tightly. So tightly, my fingers lock and my palms sweat, and it's only when we draw up outside the flat that I realise I'm still holding it.

'You should go *now*,' Yana says, looking back at Joe. 'Not safe to stay here. Good luck, Sanda. He's cold. Keep both blankets.'

'Thank you,' I say. 'Thank you for everything.'

Driving back to the inn in Natalija's car, listening to the rattle and scrape of Joe's breathing, I think about what lies ahead for me. Not just now, but forever.

Natalija's there when we arrive, her arms pressed against her sides, her face set and grim. She gasps as she sees Joe.

Peter carries him upstairs and lowers him onto a bed. Carefully, he peels back the blanket. Joe's in a bad way. He's barely conscious. His leg is bandaged but soaked with blood. What's most worrying is that he doesn't seem to recognise me. Peter finds a pair of his own pyjamas and we help Joe into them. They're too big but at least he looks more human. We leave him to sleep while Peter and Natalija go out to get some food, and I'm left to myself.

I can't help it, I go back into the room where he is, sit on a chair and watch him sleeping. His hair is beginning to grow. On his head, there's a gaping cut that's been crudely stitched.

He mutters in his sleep – nothing I can really understand – but once or twice I think I hear Andjela's name. I lean in and pull up the sheet and can't resist touching his cheek, the soft skin above his beard, and I kid myself that his eyelids pick up. I wish with all my heart that we were back in London, that none of this ever happened. I think maybe I could live with the secrets and the lies if I could have Joe.

18

Later, when Peter and Natalija get back, I'm waiting for them.

'I'm sorry,' I say, 'for everything. For what you risked. You hardly know me ...' My eyes fill up with tears.

Natalija goes straight to me and holds me.

'It's OK. It's OK, Sanda. This is our life. These people are everywhere. They listen to us. They watch us. But they won't stop us from helping our friends.'

I hug her back. When she pulls away, I see her wipe her eyes.

'Come and eat,' she says. 'We have bread and meat. When Joe wakes up, I'm going to call the UK, try to speak to his mother.'

After we've eaten, the phone rings. Peter answers and talks in a hushed tone, all the while looking over at me.

He hangs up. 'That was him, Branko. He'll be here in a couple of hours.'

My mouth is suddenly dry and my tongue burrs. I want

to cry but I can't. I can't keep still. But I can't move. Every cell, every nerve in my body is straining and twitching. I go up to see Joe. I sit on the bed and as I do, his eyes open. A kind of grin spreads itself over his face.

'Sand … my head …'

'Joe, it's so good to hear you … to see you. I'm just so happy you're here … Natalija's calling your mum … I … Oh God …'

He takes my hand and squeezes it.

'Me too,' he says and coughs, letting go of my hand. I help to prop him up on the pillow and I'm aware of his eyes on me.

'Joe … Is Andjela … I mean … did she …?'

'I don't know. She was with me when I got knocked down. I was unconscious … she must have legged it.'

He raises himself up on his elbow and looks at me. And in spite of what he's been through, the fact that he's thin and pale and broken, he's beautiful. I breathe him in.

He says, 'Thank you.'

'What for?'

'You came to get me. I … I didn't think I'd ever get out of there. They knew who I was. They were asking about you. I think they were going to …' He doesn't finish but I know because I'd feared it too. 'Those people … they're ruthless.'

'I know. I think my sister's been taken somewhere like it. When my father gets here, I'm going back up into the mountains. I'm going to find them – Senka and Andjela. I'm not giving up.'

He smiles at me and touches my hand, just lightly. Fingertips.

'I believe you.' Then he says, 'Your *father?*'

'Yeah. He's here. He's been in touch. I'm going to meet him at last. He's coming here any minute now.'

'How do you *know?*'

'How do I know what?'

'Well, how do you know it's your dad?'

'Well … I found that letter … I showed you …'

'Sanda!' Peter's calling from the living room.

'Yeah … I know that … but how do you *know* …?'

I stand up. 'Shit! Joe, I've got to go down. I'm so excited – scared too obviously – but I know it's him. I just know it! It has to be. After all we've been through. My parents … Zbrisć … Oh Joe, it's so good to have you back … I've been so worried … I mean, you've been … you were … And now I'm meeting … how do I look?'

In answer, he sits up, pulls me back down onto the bed and on top of him.

'Joe, I'll hurt you.'

'You're light as a feather.'

He puts an arm around me and brings me closer. My beanie falls over my eyes and I'm momentarily blinded. But just then everything stops because I feel his lips on my cheek, searching, loving, and then on my mouth. A lingering kiss as his dry lips open on mine and our tongues meet. I kiss him back and let myself fall into him.

After forever, he says, 'You're beautiful.'

And it's there. That moment when the world stops, and

I can hear Peter calling me but it's like he's at the end of a long railway tunnel and I don't care.

'Oh, Joe …' I kiss him again, and he cups my face in his hands.

Another call from Peter: *'Sanda! He's coming!'*

'Sanda …' says Joe

'Yes?'

'Be careful.'

I squeeze his hand and skip out of the door.

I am a leaf on water. I am drifting and floating and curling at the edges. I cannot believe how and why it's all happened in the middle of everything else but it has and I'm inside it and he's in me, and I know now that things will work out. They have to because I'm in love. For real. Peter is talking to me but I don't hear him. I gaze out of the window as a car pulls up and a tall man in dark glasses and an overcoat gets out.

My father.

He walks towards the inn, all the while talking on his phone. He has a sweep of black hair and pale skin. As he reaches the door, he hangs up. He pauses a moment, tugs at his sleeves, holds his throat.

I watch him.

And him walking to the door and me waiting is a thousand years. I hear the door opening, muffled exchanges. Already I can smell him: lemons, tar, tobacco. The room fills up with him.

And I'm face to face with my father. I'm dumb.

Peter coughs and says, 'Sanda, this is your father.'

He and Natalija step back. It's like there's a strange chalked circle around me. Branko steps into it. He hesitates for a fraction of a second. His eyes are black under heavy brows.

'So this is my beautiful daughter? I have waited so long to see you.' He puts out his hand. I take it and it closes on mine. Dry and cold. The fingers grip for a little longer than is comfortable.

'Hello,' I say shyly.

'How are you?' he says, smiling.

There's nothing in the rule book about meeting a long-lost parent. I don't know what to do, how to *be*. We stand like two wrestlers before a bout. We watch each other, and in my head, I peel under his skin, poke and pull at every hair, pinch at his cheeks.

Everyone is quiet. Then Peter says, 'Please. Sit down. Would you like a coffee?'

'No thank you.'

'Sanda?'

I just shake my head. I feel that I should be crying or dancing, rushing forward to hug him. I fiddle with my beanie, take it off and then put it back on when I see him glance at my hair.

'I … I have been searching a long time for you, Sanda,' he says.

I find my voice. 'You live in France?'

He nods.

Peter says, 'You're in Bordeaux? Are you in the centre or outside? We know it quite well. We were there on our honeymoon.'

'Yes. Yes. France is very beautiful.'

France. A letter with a French stamp on the kitchen table in London; she knew he was coming. She knew.

'Do you live with anyone? Are you …?' I falter here but I so want to know more about him.

He looks at Peter as he answers me, 'Ah. You have many questions! I will tell you all about it. We have a long journey together.'

I bring out the photograph I found in the attic in London and put it on the table in front of him.

'I brought this. I kept it with me.'

It's scratched and creased from being stuffed in endless pockets and folded and unfolded. He picks it up, turns it in his hands and bows his head.

Again he says, 'Yes … yes … A long time to search. My dear girls. I wanted to find you.'

'And my mother? What happened to my …?' and now I'm crying. Miserable little whimpers that cough themselves out of me. Natalija rubs my back.

'She died,' Branko says softly. 'In the war.'

'Oh God. Oh God!' I suppose I've known it all along. Known it, but the words break me. They wash themselves through me, over my ribs and into my heart. And again that hatred wells up for the woman who called herself my mother for all those years, for the lies she told and the bitter secrets she kept.

Branko pats my hand. 'Shall we go?' he says.

'To find your other daughter?' says Peter. 'Where will

you start? We think she might have been taken to …'

'I know where she is. I have found her. She is waiting to meet you, Sanda.'

'Senka? You found her?'

'Yes. She is safe. I have a house here. She is safe. She's waiting to see you.'

'Oh!' I look back in excitement at Peter and Natalija.

Peter steps up. 'That's marvellous news! Listen, you can stay here tonight, if you like. Start out tomorrow?'

'No. Please, I have a car. We need to go today. I have waited a long time to find my daughters. We go together.'

He takes my hand in his large paw.

Peter says, 'I'll come with you?'

Branko says, 'Not necessary.'

'But –,' he says.

'It's OK, Peter,' I say and smile. 'I'll call you when we get there. We'll come and see you. With Senka? We can do that can't we?' I ask Branko.

'Of course. Of course,' he says.

'Give me a minute,' I say and I dash upstairs to Joe's room. He's sleeping. Very gently I brush the back of his hand, against the veins like sand under his skin. I breathe him in and I go.

Peter and Natalija are at the front door. Branko's waiting by the car.

Peter scratches at his beard. 'I'm coming with you.'

'There's no need.'

'I feel responsible for you, Sanda, we both do. I can't just let you go – I've only met Branko once.'

Natalija says, 'He's a good man, Peter. I had a long talk with him yesterday. All he wants is to make up for lost time. He's told me where his house is, where Sanda's sister's waiting. He's given me the address for heaven's sake.'

He looks from her to me. 'You sure you're OK? You don't want me to come?'

I hug them both. 'I'm OK. I'm going to see my sister. This is my family!'

I go to leave but Peter holds me a little longer. 'You're *sure*?' I see a shadow arc across his face. His eyes are wide. 'You know where we are.'

'Yes, yes. I'm sure. I'll call you in a couple of hours I promise. Thank you so much for your help. I am so grateful to you,' I say.

Branko comes over, glancing at his watch. 'Come, Sanda, let's go to see your sister.'

And he walks.

And I follow him.

Away from the inn.

To find my sister.

There is a driver in the car. Branko says something to him and then joins me on the back seat. The seats are cream leather and the windows are tinted. As we pull away, Branko pats my hand again and sits back contentedly. We drive on through the countryside, and I begin to relax a little. And ask some questions. He answers me in short sentences, while he looks ahead, every so often switching to talk to the driver.

'Tell me about your home,' I say. 'Where you were brought up?'

'A small village, east of here. My father had horses.'

'Really? And you have brothers and sisters?'

'I had four brothers. All dead now.'

'I'm sorry,' I say. 'And how long have you lived in France?'

'Oh. Many years, it's a very beautiful place.'

'I've never been.'

'Oh. Yes.'

'I lived in London.'

'Yes.'

He seems irritable. Preoccupied maybe. But I'm getting frustrated. I want answers. I want to understand this man. I try to tell him a little about me, about my life in England. I even tell him about Joe. I'm about to tell him about Senka and how I found out about her, when the driver slows and turns to ask a question.

Branko leans forward to answer, and when he does, I see at the base of his neck, just below the hairline, a tattoo: a black scorpion.

19

My stomach churns. I can hear my heart pulsing in my ears and throat. Why would my father who suffered so much at the hands of the Serbs in the war, have such a potent symbol of a Serbian militia group tattooed on his neck?

And I know all at once that everything is wrong.

Branko settles back in the seat and I say, 'Where are we going exactly?'

'To see your sister.'

'Yes, but where is –?'

'You will see,' he smiles.

'Where are we going? Where are you taking me?'

'That's enough now.'

There's a sour taste in my mouth, and a tail of cold sweat creeps down my spine.

'*Who are you?* Who the fuck *are* you?'

'Quiet please.'

'You're not my father, you're *so* not my father, you're not Branko. *Who are you?*'

From the pocket of his coat, he draws a pistol and pushes it hard against my cheek. 'Be. Quiet. Please. No. No I am not Branko. My name is Goran. That is all you need to know.'

I'm quiet. I am no one again. I am nobody. I have no name. I've put the people who helped me in danger and I'm no closer to finding my sister. Tears spill quietly into my hands while he growls into his phone.

Mountains loom in the distance: dark, lumpen masses pulling the sun down behind them as we drive on. I take a calculated risk that he isn't going to shoot me just yet and say,

'You won't get away with this – you can't. People know. They'll know. They'll guess what you're doing. They'll come for me.'

'Maybe,' he says, 'but there won't be any *you* to come for, my dear.'

'My father ... Where is ...?'

'You will see in good time.'

'What are you going to do with me?'

Goran looks at me for a minute and blinks. He rubs his nose with the butt of the pistol. 'Well, I'm going to take you to meet your dear sister like I told you.'

I've been a fool, a desperate, gullible child.

I try to console myself with the fact that Joe's OK, that his mum will be on her way. He'll go home, back to London to live a normal life, play in his band, go to school, get a girlfriend and forget about me. And a year down the line, no one will even remember who I was.

The car drives off the road down a dark tree-lined avenue. A deer starts in the headlights and jumps the fence at the side of the track. An old stone house comes into view, the windows black and blind, only a single light coming from the front porch. The car stops and the driver gets out and opens my door. Goran's still pointing the gun at me as I slide across the seat and out into the cold night air. There's a crust of frost on the ground that crackles like glass under my feet. He ushers me up the steps to the door and pushes it open.

We're standing in a vast hall under the gaze of at least forty pairs of eyes. Stags' heads of different shapes and sizes watch us as we cross the floor. Opposite the door is a large staircase. Up we go: one, then two flights as it twists round away from the hall, the gun always at my back if I slow down. It's stiflingly hot in the house and I'm roasting in my hat and coat.

It's funny because I don't feel scared any more. I just feel sort of resigned. I want an end to this mad journey now. But what I want more than ever is to understand who I am and where I come from. The fact that it's probably going to get me killed is kind of on the back burner at the moment. And Joe kissed me, and it felt so good. That's what I try to think about.

We're on the second floor now and we both pause for breath. To my left, I see a long passage, carpeted in blue and red swirls, that yawns away towards a high arched window where it bellies out into a small landing lit by a crystal chandelier. Under this, I see two people deep in conversation. They hear us and look up but they make no move towards us. One is a man wearing a dark jumper and a shoulder holster; the other, tall and bony with bleached hair that fizzes in the light like nylon, is my 'mother' – Kristina.

Goran makes a sign to her and she nods sharply. We go on up another narrow flight on bare boards to the top of the house. A long, sloping corridor hung about with cobwebs stretches to the left of us. He switches on a dim bulb and I pick my way along past broken chairs and tea crates full of old china. At the end of the corridor, on the left, is a small door. There's a key in the lock and he leans past me, turns it and throws open the door.

I peer in and around the room. As I do so, he shoves me inside, pulls the door shut and turns the key in the lock. The room is lit by another single low watt bulb. There's an iron bedstead covered with a heap of blankets, a listing rocking chair and a cracked sink in the corner.

As his footsteps fall away, the heap of blankets moves and stirs and from underneath it, a figure crawls out trailing dust and fluff: my sister.

It's unmistakeable. Like a bee sting, like soap in your eyes. It actually hurts to be close to her. She sloughs off the covers, gets down off the bed and stands to face me.

We stare at each other for a long time. I hold out my hand to her and she moves a little closer. I notice she walks with a kind of stoop as though she's been carrying something heavy on one side forever. Her hair is a bit longer than mine and she's very thin. She's wearing a dirty nightdress that's about ten sizes too big for her.

I whisper, 'Senka?'

She comes towards me and holds out her hands. Her fingers when they touch me feel like plastic. I scan her face and mark every line: her nose, the curve of her brows and, of course, her eyes. My own face gazes back at me, my own eyes: one green, one blue. My sister. My family.

We nestle together on the bed under one of the dusty blankets and I try to engage her in conversation. All the while, from below, we can hear noises: bangs and clatters, like something being mended or broken.

Senka speaks in a hoarse whisper, and I have to lean in to hear her at times. It's like she isn't used to speaking or being listened to. She seems to find it difficult at first but with gentle encouragement, she manages to continue.

I find out she's been in the orphanage at Zbrisć for most of her life; while I was going to school in London, she was caged in that awful place.

I ask her about school. She says she's had only a little basic schooling from a local priest, no books or toys. She tells me she was ten when she was put to work in the kitchens, scrubbing floors, peeling endless blackened potatoes, and fetching and carrying for the staff.

I ask her how she came to be here, and with her eyes fixed on me, she tells me she'd heard of it before. All the kids at Zbrisć knew about the House. She echoes what the pig farmer told me:

'This is where they send you if you are bad — you never come back.'

She tells me how, the night after we escaped, they brought her here. She shows me her arm. It's covered in welts and bruises.

I ask her, 'Did Goran do this to you?'

She shakes her head: '*Kristina.*' My fake mother. I feel sick.

'How did she know about the orphanage?'

'They're sisters,' she says.

'*Who?*'

'Kristina and Madame Milanković.'

'*Christ.*'

All those years.

Kristina must have been talking to Milanković about Senka, and I never knew a thing. I grip Senka's hand and force myself to think it through. Why has Kristina brought us both here? Together? Why keep us apart all this time and then do this? None of it makes sense.

'Senka, do you remember our mother?' I say gently.

She remembers us being pulled away from our mother's arms, bundled together onto a truck by a man, then later, in a car, a woman in the back seat catching hold of her with long hands around her middle. She remembers screaming and kicking to get away. She says that at one point she kicked at the woman so violently, there was blood on her face. She remembers the woman howling in pain, spitting blood, then hitting her hard over and over again.

So that's how Kristina lost her front teeth.

She remembers the day I left the orphanage: summer, the grass wilting in the heat, a dead cat, a stew of blowflies, and the sound of her fists against a high window. She remembers looking down and my face over someone's shoulder. She never forgot it.

She wants to know about me, so I tell her my story so far. She sits very close to me, and listens intently with her head on one side. Sometimes she brushes her hand against my cheek. I understand. I feel the same need to touch her, to make sure this is real. I tell her of our escape and how I'd seen her at the window that night.

'You saved me,' I say. 'The dog? That was you, wasn't it? How?'

She nods, and the ghost of a smile crosses her face and fades.

'I saw you the first time you were brought to Zbrisć but they kept me away – put me to work in the boys' quarters – they watched me closely,' she says. 'But that night there was chaos, noise, the dogs barking: they left the door unlocked … I looked out and saw you there. I didn't think. I went quickly, took scissors from the kitchen, slipped through the coal door by the kitchen – no one saw me – and I stabbed it.'

'You were brave.'

She smiles. 'No.'

'We should have taken you with us.'

'I would have slowed you down. I'm not strong,' she says.

'I came back for you. I came back to find you,' I say.

'To find me,' she whispers.

I'm just getting to the bit about the letter and the

photograph from Branko when I hear footsteps in the corridor. We fall quiet as the key grinds in its lock.

Goran stands in the doorway. He's changed from his business suit into overalls. He has on rubber boots and thick socks turned over them at the knee. At his neck he wears a woollen scarf tied in a kind of bow.

He takes out his gun and points it. 'Come with me.'

Senka scrabbles to her feet and, with head bowed meekly, goes to him. I can see her shape through the formless shift she wears, the jut of her hips and her backbone like a chain.

I take my time. I shrug off my coat and put it around Senka. As I do so, she raises her eyes to me with a little smile of gratitude.

He watches us with a sneer. 'Nice touch. But you won't need it for long.' He seems to find this very funny and chuckles to himself. 'Out!'

'Where are we going?' I ask.

'For a walk in the woods. Now be quiet – do like your sister.'

'If we're going outside, she needs some shoes.'

'What?'

'She needs something on her feet!'

I think for a moment he's going to hit me but instead he turns, rummages around in a tea chest, and brings out a pair of carpet slippers in a lurid shade of green. He throws them at her, and she ducks instinctively. It makes me think of Andjela. I want to go to her and hold her, to protect her from everything and everyone, but I wait.

She picks up the slippers and puts them on. With a shy look at me, she follows Goran down the corridor and down the stairs to where God knows what awaits us.

20

Downstairs, in the hall, Kristina is waiting in a high-backed armchair, her hands folded in her lap, eyes closed. Goran nudges us towards her. Her eyes snap open.

'So here you are.' She speaks in Serbian. 'Together. Just what you wanted.' She looks at me. 'And what do you think of your sister?'

I say nothing. But I glare straight at her. She's wearing lipstick, and the red has leeched into the creases around her mouth. 'You didn't know your own flesh and blood was a filthy little peasant?' My anger stops up my throat like gristle. I choke it down.

Senka looks up at her, then at me. 'I ... I ...' she stutters.

'You —,' Kristina picks at a back tooth, delicately, with her little finger held high, turns a lazy eye on Senka, 'you don't speak to me or look at me. Do you understand?'

'Don't talk to her like that,' I say.

Kristina's head jerks around: 'How *dare* you? You thankless little *bitch*,' she spits. 'God, how did I put up

with you all that time? All those years. The smell of you,
your voice, your whining.'

'My *voice*? You hardly spoke to me!'

'Shut up. I took you. I paid for it. Every fucking day.
You saw to that.'

'*Why then?* Why did you do it?'

Here she smiles. 'Why? That's a good question. Why
does anyone do anything? For money? For love?'

'*Love?*' I say. 'You don't know the meaning of the word.'

At that, she lurches up and slaps me hard across my face
with the flat of her hand, then sits back down, smoothing
her skirt. But I'm not afraid of her any more. The truth
— hers and mine — has set me free and spinning. I feel
powerful. For the first time in my life.

'You have no idea about me. No idea about my life,'
she says.

'I know more than you think. I know what you did
in the War.'

She flattens her back against the chair. 'Oh. That.
And you think *you* can judge me now? You don't know
anything. You know *nothing* about it. War is hard and it's
dirty and it's complicated. No one is innocent. *No one.*'

I ask again, 'Why *did* you take me?'

'I told you why.'

'You *loved* me?'

She purses her mouth in disgust. 'I didn't *love* you. You
were *nothing* to me. You were like … like an animal, like
a mule. You had a job to do and you've done it. It's over.
That's why you're here.'

'A *job* …?'

'Yes. You were doing a job; both of you. You were helping me punish someone. Dragan too – he was a part of it until he started to care about you and make a fuss.'

'He's dead.'

She shrugs. 'That's what happens when you start to think you can change things.'

'He wrote me a letter. I think he loved you.'

'Weak,' she says. 'Let me ask you. Where do you think *strength* really comes from? What gives a man the *strength* to go on, to endure?'

'I don't know.'

'No, you wouldn't. *She* might though.' She gestures to Senka. 'I'll tell you. It is *hope*. You take away *hope* from a person and they're empty: weak and empty.'

Kristina claps her hands and a low door is opened in the wall. Two men come into the room, dragging someone between them. His head hangs limply and his bare feet leave a thin wash of blood on the floor behind him. They manoeuvre him into a chair near Kristina, stand behind him, and one of them pulls back his head by his hair. He has a high, lined brow, even features and gold-green eyes that fill with tears as they meet mine. Right away, I feel something: a kind of force, a tiny pulse inside me that sets up a soft beat against my heart. At my side, Senka reaches for my hand.

He struggles to move but they have him pinned into the chair by his arms.

Kristina flicks her eyes at him and goes on: 'I had hope once. Hope *and* love. Yes, *me*. But that was taken from me.

An eye for an eye. This man,' she gestures in his direction, 'took my love, *my hope.*'

'No,' I hear from the man in the chair.

At once, she walks over to face him, bends and places a finger on his lips. She glances at me over her shoulder. 'And I did the same to him. That's fair isn't it?'

'Who is …?' I say, although I'm sure I know the answer. I'm holding Senka's hand so tightly, I can feel the web of tiny bones start to give.

'This is your father,' she says. 'This is Branko Hadžić.'

'Sanda, Senka, my God …' he gasps.

'And *you* – ?' I begin.

'Here he is,' says Kristina. 'And here you are. I wanted to show him one last time what he had and what he lost. He has nothing. I've *drained* him of everything, little by little.'

His eyes on her are pleading. She speaks to me. 'You think you've had a hard time? Let me tell you a story, Sanda, about a girl not much older than you and what was done to her.'

Kristina sits back down, squeezes her hands together until her knuckles glow white. Branko twitches in his chair.

She waits a moment, then: 'This girl was beautiful. She had soft skin and long blonde hair tied in a thick plait down her back. She came from nothing: from darkness, from pain. Her parents were ignorant, stupid, cold. They were jealous of her beauty, of the joy she saw in life. They kept pigs, they grew beet. That was all they had.

'But she was clever. She had a hunger for knowledge,

for learning. She wanted to be a teacher. She worked hard and she got a place at college. It was there that she met him. He was a young professor. He was tall, good looking, all the girls liked him, but he took a special interest in her. Oh yes.' She looks across at Branko, who keeps his body still and taut.

'As soon as she walked into his class on the first day, she knew he loved her, he couldn't help himself. They talked for hours after class, walked in the gardens. He sent her letters, little notes. He taught her to love, she who had known no love in her life.'

Branko shakes his head. 'It was all in your head. There was nothing between us. You're lying!' And to us, 'She's lying. I was kind to her, that's all – I felt sorry for her, but she's a monster, she's not ...'

'Gag him,' she says quietly. A filthy rag is fastened around his mouth and he slumps back. She looks at me and her eyes burn. 'Yes. We were passionate lovers, thrown together.'

Branko's shaking his head again.

'I *adored* him,' she goes on, ignoring him. 'I would have walked through fire for him. I had so much love in my heart. So much hope. Can you imagine? *Can you understand?* But then he threw it all away on some Bosniak slut, another teacher. And all those promises we'd made to each other, all my hopes, were turned into dust.'

'So, you –?'

'The war had started. I joined the Serbian Radical Party then and I lost them for a while. I heard they'd had

twin girls. And then in 1995, I saw her by chance on the
Potočari road with a group of other women and children.
And there you were – you and your idiot sister. And there
and then I decided what I was going to do. I had Dragan
shoot your mother and we took you both. But not before
I told her why. She knew who I was.

'I found *him* later in a transit camp. It was providence. I
had him transferred to my camp and before I locked him up,
I told him what I'd done, and how I was leaving the country.'

'And Dragan? He went along with all this?'

'Of course. I owned Dragan. He would have done
anything for me.'

'So what happened? What did you do?'

'Branko stayed in prison for a long time, five years or
more, long after the war ended. I saw to it from England.
I wanted him where I could find him, you see. And every
so often I would send him a little present.'

'Present?' I say.

'Photographs. Of you … and her. I wanted him to know
you were alive, growing up far away, having forgotten him;
that he was never going to see you. I made sure they kept
him alive. They had to watch him very closely. Many times
he tried to take his own life but they stopped him. He'd
still be in there but there was a change at the top and he
appealed and they had to let him go.'

'And he found you?'

'He was getting very close. They warned me. Then I
had a letter, and I knew it was time – time to return, to
wait. He got to the house in London soon after we left,

then he went to Zbrisć. He was easy to catch,' she says. 'I just told him I had you. I knew he'd come.'

I look at Branko. His eyes are brimming with tears again, and his shoulders are heaving. I go to him.

'Keep away!' She thrusts her chin at Goran, and he grabs me. 'So,' she says to Branko. 'I thought you would like to see them one last time. Just so you know I kept them alive but apart. They've grown up not knowing each other, not knowing love, or kindness, or hope. Just as I did. You remember what I wrote to you when you betrayed me, that I would never let you forget?'

Senka is looking at Kristina with absolute hatred. I try to go to Branko again but Goran holds me back, nearly tearing my arm from its socket.

'Please?' I say. '*Please* let me talk to him! *Please?*'

Suddenly, Branko pushes himself off the chair and onto his knees. I feel Goran loosen his grip, distracted. We rush towards Branko, he opens his arms and just for a moment, his hands are on my hair.

'Take them!' Kristina shouts. We're wrenched apart and taken out, leaving my father struggling between the two men. My throat is cracked from screaming.

Outside, it's pitch dark: the only light comes from the porch lamp where drowsy moths bat and whirl, their wide, patterned wings making strange shadows against the stone steps.

The car that brought me is gone. In its place is a pick-up truck. Goran shunts us over and gestures to us to get in. We stumble up the step into the trailer and turn to face him as he climbs up. He holds a length of coarse rope. Standing there in the back of the truck, looking down at the ground, I'm back in that dream. I can see it so clearly. It was in a truck like this that we'd been taken from our mother at the side of the road. I can see the woods behind her; I can see her agonised face, pleading, calling. I can see her as she falls.

Goran's binding the whiskery rope around us. He's pushing us down so we sit back to back tightly bound. A fury like I've never known rises up in me and I know if I can harness it, control it, I can beat this man. I'm determined not to go quietly.

When he's satisfied with his job, he climbs in and starts the engine, and the headlights illuminate the forest around us. I see the brightness of a rabbit's eyes caught for a moment in the glare. I stroke Senka's hand as she sits stiffly at my back. I wonder what's going on in her head. She's hardly made a sound since he came for us.

The sharp sweet smell of pine surrounds us, and leaves dip and brush our heads as we pass. We're on a narrow track taking us deep into the forest. An owl cries overhead and there's the odd movement in the undergrowth as an animal runs for cover before us. In the cab up front, music is playing and I can just hear him tapping along to the refrain on the steering wheel. After a short while, we stop at a place where the trees have thinned out around a patch of scrubby ground. He gets out of the cab and pulls out a torch and a spade.

'Shit!' I breathe.

He comes around to the back of the truck and jumps up to face us. He sets the torch down pointing at us, and proceeds to untie me and bind up Senka again. She doesn't utter a sound, her head still bowed, with its mad spikes of tawny hair shining in the torchlight.

He hands me the spade and goes to jump down, hauling me with him. 'You dig. You are stronger.'

'What for?'

'Just do it!' He turns the torch on me, and I set to work.

In spite of the cold, the ground is reasonably soft here, and I manage to clear away several clods before I hit compacted earth and rock. I get to my knees then, and start to pull up the rocks with my hands. I'm trying not to think about what I'm doing and why. I'm trying to think of what it would take to swing the spade and what damage I could do to his fat face.

I need to distract him – to bring him closer.

'How deep?'

'What?'

'How deep has this got to be?'

He looks at me and says in a matter of fact voice, 'Deep enough for two of you.'

I try again. 'I can't get this rock out. Can you help me?'

'You not used to hard work? I should maybe get your sister.'

'No! No. It's OK. I can do it. Can you bring the torch closer?'

In answer, he simply points it into my face which makes things worse. It means I can't see him.

I reach for the spade and dig on with him watching, and after what feels like hours, I have a reasonable hole, about six feet across and a foot deep. I get to my feet and brush myself down.

'Good,' he says, and he motions to me to climb down into it.

I keep looking at Senka, who sits motionless. He goes back to her, wrestles her bindings and lifts her unresisting body down.

He pushes her at me and I catch her as she stumbles in next to me.

Goran smiles. 'Very touching. Twins. Twins with the strange eyes. I remember when they took you. I said it was a bad idea. I said they should shoot you like they shot your mother.'

'You bastard!'

'Bosniak animals. Filthy pigs. She had eyes like yours too. They shot her in the face.'

All around, the forest whistles and blows. And in the light from the torch, I watch a black beetle crawl out from under a leaf. I reach for Senka's hand and I clutch it. Her fingers feel cold and dry and brittle.

She squeezes back and under her breath, she says my name: 'Sanda. *Sestra*: sister.'

Now I know it doesn't matter what happens. I have my sister, my family. And in my head, and on my skin, my father's touch. His breath.

Goran pulls out his gun and takes aim. I close my eyes. I have no fear at this moment. I've come so far and I have my sister. I cling to her and wait for death.

Nothing happens. Nothing happens.

Then a crash.

I open my eyes. First, I see the torch on the ground, its thin beam raking the dirt. Then I see him. He's lying face down, bleeding from a deep wound in the back of his head. I reach for the torch and turn it on, the gloom of the forest behind him. And, standing there, I see someone I thought I'd never see again.

'Andjela!' She looks like some kind of woodland creature. She's covered in bracken and mud, her clothes torn and threadbare but she's smiling.

'How did you find us ...?' I ask.

Slowly, she tells me: 'After Joe was taken, I went back to Zbrisć.' She looks up at me and then away into the forest. 'I had nowhere else to go.'

'Oh, Andjela,' I say.

'They said I hurt Mirko – he nearly died. They said I was to be punished. I was so frightened. They took me to the House but I escaped. I've been out here ever since.' And in an echo of Senka's words in the attic: 'Everyone knows this house. Everyone is frightened to be sent there. That woman ...'

'I know,' I say.

'I saw the headlights, heard voices.'

I swallow, think of Mirko: the glass in my hand, the soft push of flesh and muscle, the dark arc of his blood.

'They blamed you for Mirko. Andjela, I'm so sorry.'

She shrugs. 'It's OK. But you – you have your sister.

You've found each other. I'm happy for you.'

'Thank you,' I say.

Senka smiles.

'But we're wasting time,' says Andjela. I clamber up onto level ground and help Senka out. Andjela's already making for the truck.

Suddenly, I find I can't move. It's like the roots of the pines have wormed into me and I'm fixed to the ground. Andjela calls back urgently, 'Come on!'

I wake up. We hurry to the truck and I climb into the driver's seat and feel down for the keys as I've seen people do. They're still in the ignition. From a few feet away, I hear a groan and shine the torch towards the noise. He's lying at an odd angle in the dead leaves, his head a sticky mass of congealing blood, but on one hand the fingers are beginning to twitch and grope. Beyond him, I see the gun. No time to go back for it now. I turn the key and his lousy music booms out into the forest. I switch it off and after hammering several times at the pedals and gears, the truck leaps forward, then stalls and stops so abruptly that Senka bangs her head on the dashboard.

He's on his feet now, swaying, blundering towards us like a zombie. He throws himself across the bonnet and bellows. Senka cowers in the front seat.

Andjela nudges me and says, 'Come on Sanda.'

It's down to me and I know it. I have one more chance to make this work. I switch the engine on again, shove my left foot at one of the pedals I'm guessing is the clutch, crank the gear stick, and eventually manage to thrust the truck into gear. We lurch forward – enough to throw him off the bonnet – and after two or three starts and stops, I find the accelerator pedal. I figure the braking bit will just come to me later. Right now, we need to be moving. And we are, cutting back through the track in the forest.

I momentarily take my eye off the path ahead and we slam into a tree. The bonnet buckles and steam starts to cloud out into the cold air.

'Shit! *Shit!*'

I try the key and nothing happens. What an idiot! As far as I can see at this point, we have two choices: we can either sit here in the dark with the doors locked, or get out and run like hell. We choose the latter. I open my door and we jump down.

We set off through the forest with the bracken clawing and winding at our legs. I look over my shoulder to see he's gaining on us.

We have to face him. End him. End this. A little further on up ahead, the ground slopes away into a kind of trench. I make for it, frantically beckoning for them to follow. We tumble into the trench and into a slush of wet leaves and mulch in the bottom.

'OK?' I ask Senka.

'Yes. Yes I'm OK.'

'Andjela?'

She nods, looking back anxiously.

To myself more than anyone else, I say: 'Ambush. We're going to have to ambush him. We need a stick. A big stick.'

I look about. At the top of the trench, snaking towards us like a long arm is such a stick. I grab it and pull it but it won't budge. On tiptoes, in freezing mush, I waggle it backwards and forwards until it begins to splinter from its mooring. It breaks away with a creaking sound, leaving the end sharp and jagged. Perfect.

I can hear him now, his heavy panting. We crouch low, and wait. And wait. When he's nearly on top of us, I stand up brandishing the stick and shove it square into his face. He staggers back and I'm out of the trench in an instant. I hit him again and again. He sinks to his knees, covering his eyes, his face streaked with blood. And again I raise the stick: it's like I can't stop, I can't feel anything any more but this.

'That's enough,' Andjela says.

But I find I can't let go of the stick. My fingers are clasped so tightly, they're stuck, frozen around it. She tugs at the stick and reluctantly, I let it go.

We move on fast, leaving Goran's unconscious body behind. Ahead, I can make out traces of headlights from the road below.

And what now? Where now?

I try to think. But thinking is hard because I'm shaking, from my fingertips through my whole body. And I can't stop it and I can't think straight. I can see his face slacken and cave as I bring down the stick.

When we get to the road, I have to stop. I'm still trembling, and I sit down at the side of the road and wait for Andjela and Senka to catch up. Andjela puts her hand on my arm and squeezes it. I look up at her. She's survived so much. She gives me hope that we'll get through this too. And that's enough for me.

I get to my feet. 'I'm OK. We need to keep moving.'

We have to get to the inn, the Ship. We need help to go back for Branko.

I look about me. We're at the edge of what looks like a small village. I can just make out the chop and curl of tiled roofs. And, here and there, bars of yellow light from the houses. The nights out here are so different from London. It's like swimming underwater, a rich coal-black soup of dark that presses on my eyes and ears.

Headlights. We fall flat on the verge as a car passes us. The driver is listening to music, tapping out the beat on the wheel, his mouth frozen in an 'O' as he sings.

We sit back up. I look dubiously at Senka's slippers. They're torn and matted. Both girls look exhausted. But there's nothing for it. We have to go on.

I try to remember Peter's village. The road by the river, the cobble-stones on the bridge, the twin white churches; and then the inn, with the crooked balcony over the water.

It's enough. It has to be. But can we get there before Kristina does? She must know I've got nowhere else to go. I need to get to a telephone. I need to warn them.

I get up. Andjela and Senka are still sitting together a little way off, leaning on each other. Senka is examining her feet, pulsing them between thumb and finger. I go over and take a look. In the faint light, I see a blue fan of bones. Her toenails are broken and the soles of her feet are raw. I hold them and I see her thrill for a moment at the warmth from my hands. I have nothing to bind them with but I take off my socks and give them to her. Andjela collects a handful of grass and together we stuff the slippers to make them fit. We help her up and we set off.

We walk through the village, hugging the walls, staying out of the light. We see no one. A cat on a wall mews as we pass, and we leave the place as quietly as we came. We go on, with the forest on one side, reaching up to the mountains beyond, and fields on the other. And far away in the distance, there's the silver-green cut of a river.

We carry on through the night, keeping close to the road until dawn breaks. Then we cut back into the forest where the land starts to climb over moss and roots and rocks like shoulders sticking out of the ground. I see a deer bending to eat higher up. It starts at our approach, its black nose dusted with moss, and disappears into the trees. Andjela stops and puts her finger to her lips. We all listen. Water.

'Where?' I say.

She smiles and points upwards. We climb towards the noise. A hunchback of grass and stone, and water pouring down from its head into a stream. There are icicles like meat hooks hanging further up, and beyond them is a kind of hollow.

Andjela scrabbles up to it and calls back, 'Come on!'

I help Senka up. It's a tiny cave, not more than a few feet wide, but big enough for us to rest for a while. We've been walking for at least nine hours without a break. I look at Andjela: her face is freckled blue by early sun and shade. She's tired, but she's fired up. There's a kind of defiance, fierceness about her, but I'm worried about my sister. Andjela finds a scoop of bark and we take it in turns to collect water from the falls to bathe her feet and her poor head. She seems feverish. I'm scared because I know how far we have to travel. The slippers are now shredded. I remove them carefully, put them on, and give her my shoes. We make a moss pillow for her, I stroke her head, and she's asleep at once.

21

'She's sick,' Andjela says.

'I know. I know,' I say.

After an hour or so, we have to wake her. And for a minute she doesn't seem to know where she is or even who we are. Her head is hot and her face is flushed.

'Senka! Senka! *Come on*!' we say. I help her on with my shoes. Leaning on us, she gets to her feet, swaying and muttering to herself.

'We must get some food,' says Andjela.

She's right. I know she's right. We're all hungry but I feel if Senka doesn't eat soon, she's not going to make it.

We limp back down towards the road, and Andjela and I take Senka's weight. At the roadside, we have to stop as she loses consciousness and hangs between us like a rag doll. We look at each other, and Andjela steps into the road with her arm extended.

We don't have to wait long. Senka lies in my arms, slipping in and out of the world, as Andjela flags down a car. I see her lean in and beg for help. I see the driver's look of undisguised disgust.

He spits out the word *'Roma'*, closes the window and waves her away.

She turns to me with a shrug and it's then that I lay Senka down and go and stand with Andjela. We have better luck the next time: a farmer's pick-up. The driver lets us into the back among sacks of potatoes and a sheepdog with a collar of frayed string. Then, with a glance at Senka, he goes to his cab and brings out bread and a bottle of what looks like whisky. Andjela cradles her head while we encourage her to drink. It brings her round at once, coughing. I break the bread and feed it to her, piece by tiny piece, like you'd feed a bird, and she rallies a little.

'Thank you very much!' we say.

I ask him about the inn called the Ship on the river near the white churches. He knows it. He can take us to Libač, about fifty kilometres from the inn. From there, he's going north.

It's bitterly cold in the back of the truck and after a while, the farmer stops and pulls over. He lifts Senka out and puts her in the warm cab with him and covers her with his jacket. Andjela and I huddle up under sacking and try to sleep. At Libač, by a red brick school with a tall bell tower, he lets us out, giving us directions for the inn.

We cannot thank him enough and there are tears in my eyes as he says goodbye. Before he goes, he reaches into his pocket, pulls out a banknote and hands it awkwardly to me. Then he takes off his jacket and gives it to Senka. We wave vigorously as he drives away.

The first thing we do is find a shop that sells food. We buy bread and honey, a bottle of sickly sweet juice and some tea towels to use as bandages for Senka's feet.

Afterwards, I can see Senka's better for the food but she's still very frail. We have fifty kilometres to go and it's a straight road south following the river. As we leave, it starts to rain. The slippers have disintegrated: my feet are torn and bleeding from the rasp of tarmac but I can't feel them any more. We spend the night in an empty barn near the road, curled up together for warmth, and leave at daybreak.

Another day's walking. We're soaked through and weary but something keeps us moving. Every so often, we rest and eat. We've spent all the money and we've eaten most of the food. We tramp on for the rest of the day until it's dark.

Then I see it. 'Look!'

Up ahead, the white spire of the first church looms, and across the river are the lights of the Ship.

We cross the bridge, sliding on wet stones, the river coursing beneath us. The air is iron and salt. I think of Joe. His hands are on my back, his voice in my ear and his lips on my neck; I'm walking for him, to him. And I have my sister.

It's taken us nearly three days to get here.

On the other side, by the twin church, I stop. Fear catches in my throat, it winds me. I kneel in the wet grass and the river bellies and sings, and in its reaches, I see lit windows and the bleached bone steeple from the church on the opposite bank. I hold my head.

Senka comes to me. 'Sanda?' she says softly, and she combs my hair with her fingers. 'Sanda?'

'OK. I'm OK,' I say.

We walk along the river, past the well, the dark huddle of houses, and come to a stop at the door of the inn.

The door is opened by Natalija.

She holds out her arms. 'Sanda!'

'I'm sorry,' I say. 'I'm so sorry.'

'I should never have let you go. *Never.* Peter said he should go and I stopped him. I'm so sorry.'

The skin around her eyes is lined and pouchy, and her hands are cold. 'This is your sister?'

'Yes. This is Senka, and this is …'

I turn, but Andjela's no longer behind me. Her slight, hunched figure is moving quickly away, crossing the square towards the bridge.

'Andjela!' I call.

She doesn't look back and I know I have to go after her. I leave Senka and race across the cobbles towards her. I catch up with her easily and grab hold of her hand.

'Andjela! What are you doing? Where are you going?'

'No police!'

'But there won't be police! No police. I promise. I promise, Andjela. It's OK …'

We stand together for a moment, wet through and out of breath. She shakes her head, then bursts into heaving sobs, and I see just how frightened she is. I understand I have to let her come of her own accord. I release her hand and stand back. I say, 'I won't let anything happen. I promise ... No police. No Zbrisć. I promise ...Andjela?'

Of course, at that moment I don't know exactly what awaits us but I do know I'm not going to let any of us go back there. Ever.

Her body relaxes and her arms fall. She even begins to move towards me. But then her eyes fix on a spot behind me: they widen in fear, and she turns to run. I look over my shoulder; Peter is coming towards us, he's saying something but his voice is lost in the wind. I say, 'They're friends, Andjela. They're friends.'

She seems unsure of what to do. She turns, trips on a paving stone and loses her footing. At once, Peter is there. She covers her head with her arms as I saw her do back in Zbrisć. He picks her up like a child and speaks to her in soothing words. The fight has left her. She's too exhausted to do anything other than lean into his chest as he carries her back into the inn.

Inside, Natalija asks, 'Is this your friend from Zbrisć?'

'This is Andjela. She saved our lives.'

'Andjela,' she says it so sweetly, 'and your sister: you brought her back.'

'Senka. Is she OK?'

'She's upstairs. She's very weak. I'm making some soup. Peter's closing the inn.'

The smell of thyme and roast tomatoes fills the room.

Peter sets Andjela down and she comes to stand by me.

I say, 'Andjela's so scared of being sent back ... I've tried, but ... will you tell her it's OK?'

'Of course,' says Peter.

'Thank you,' I say, and my mind's humming. I blurt out in a rush of excitement because I can almost see it now: 'I guess Senka and I can maybe go to England. I mean ... there might be foster families ... you know ... and I was thinking, she could go to my school. The government will look after us, won't they?'

Peter says, 'Let's see.'

Natalija offers her hand to Andjela. 'Come with me?'

She says it so gently, and her smile's so bright, that after a moment's hesitation, Andjela lets herself be led upstairs, leaving me with Peter.

I know there's so much more to talk about, but I can't help myself: 'Is Joe −?'

He shakes his head. 'He's back in the UK. His mother flew over when we called her. She insisted she take him back and I don't blame her. He was so worried about you. He tried to get away and go after you. But she stopped him − she couldn't risk losing him again. He's in hospital − an infection − I spoke with her yesterday. He's left a letter for you.'

A letter.

'Where is it?'

'Sanda ...' says Peter.

'Hmm?' My head is full of Joe again.

'I wanted to say how sorry I was. How the hell could I have let you just walk out of here with the first guy that waltzes up saying he's your father? I'm an idiot. A total idiot. I should have insisted.'

'It wasn't you. I wanted to believe it ...' I falter and look at him. He shakes his head.

I go on, 'I thought Kristina might have come for you. I was so frightened.'

He beckons me into the kitchen and busies himself with the soup. He brings out a bulging loaf dusted with flour, and slices a hunk for me as he talks.

'You were gone about two or three hours before I started to get really twitchy. Natalija too. There was something about him that – I don't know – on reflection just didn't feel right. We waited until we just couldn't sit still any longer and then I knew what I had to do. I went to Zbrisć. To the orphanage.'

'You saw it?'

'God.' He's straining the tomatoes. 'God, Sanda. What a place.'

'You met her – Milanković?'

'After a struggle, yes. And I put it to her that I knew everything, all about what was going on, and that I was in touch with some very powerful international forces – wasn't too specific – but it did the job. She rolled over. Told me where you'd been taken.'

'I don't believe it.'

'I think she knows the game's up for her. I've been in touch with the authorities about Zbrisć, said if they don't do something about it, every TV crew in the northern hemisphere will be descending on them. I went there that night – to the house – with some pals of mine, ex-army, ex-UN, and, well … it's … there are basically dungeons in the basement. It's sordid. We found six people down there, starving and abused, two certainly from Zbrisć.'

'And my father?'

But he carries on. 'Being sent to the house was obviously the ultimate threat at Zbrisć.' I can hear Natalija on the stairs now. He says, 'Kristina's in custody. She's wanted for war crimes, and I wouldn't mind guessing that she's been overseeing the goings-on in that house from England. She won't get out for a long time.'

'And …?'

Natalija comes into the room and shoots a look at Peter. 'Soup ready?' she says brightly. 'The girls are resting. Senka's going to be OK, Sanda, but she's malnourished and completely exhausted. I don't know how you made it, I really don't.'

'I should go to her …' I say.

Again, that look between them. She says, 'In a minute. I'll take them some soup.'

'Sanda, there's someone we want you to meet,' says Peter.

Natalija opens the door at the back of the kitchen on to a small room. She stands aside for me to go in. The room is dimly lit by a little stove in a corner, flames dancing and crackling in its belly.

A man is standing by the window, partly in shadow. I know him at once.

22

Smiling, he takes a step towards me. 'Sanda.'

Instinctively, I back away. Slowly. The stone is cold under my feet. My toes lift away from it.

No one speaks. Natalija goes to leave but I stop her. I look at him. His green-gold eyes are tired and his skin is waxy and bruised. 'Sanda?' He speaks very softly. 'I'm Branko. Your friends are brave. They got me out of there.'

His voice is like a song you hear from years ago, that you thought you'd forgotten until you hear it again. And you know all the words – every one. His voice was already inside my head. It's been there all along. I just never knew it until now.

I'm crying now, and I look at my father and he has tears in his eyes too.

'I must get Senka,' I say.

Natalija says, 'No, wait. She's been through so much. Let her rest a little.'

He speaks again. 'All these years, I've thought of

nothing but you and your sister. When I got out of prison, I went all over, every children's home, every church, every school. I put ads in the newspapers but there were so many, so many looking for daughters, sons, fathers.' He pauses and checks himself.

'Those photographs?' I whisper.

He nods. 'Yes. Every so often an envelope would be put into my cell with a photo and a date on the back. It used to crucify me. Of you, of Senka too: thin and pale in rags. Every time, I'd will myself not to open the envelopes, but I always knew I'd have to in the end. And you were growing up, every year that passed, getting further and further away from me, from what you'd known.'

Natalija says, 'So cruel.'

He smiles at Natalija and turns back to me: 'What Kristina told you, back there, in the house, it wasn't true. I never led her on. I was never in love with her. I was *kind* to her, that's all; she'd had a difficult life. It was just some stupid infatuation. At least that's what I thought.'

He puts his hands on my shoulders. 'Look. I understand you're scared. You don't know who to trust any more. But I can show you papers. I can *prove* I am who I say I am – whatever you want. But … I would like to … can I tell you? My story? What happened to me and how you were lost.'

'Yes please.'

Natalija says: 'Please sit down. I'll leave you to talk.'

There are two armchairs, one either side of the stove. I sit facing my father.

'When you and your sister were born, it was the happiest time of my life. There were complications. Twins are difficult sometimes but you were healthy, and your mother ...! When you were put into her arms, she was more beautiful than ever. She made all your clothes: dresses, little jackets and hats – all the same. We were very happy. Around the time you and your sister were born, we were living in a little town outside Srebrenica. It was in Eastern Bosnia. We are Bosniaks, you see, Bosnian Muslims. The Serbs wanted to gain independence, and to do that Srebrenica was important for them. They wanted to take it. To make it theirs. You understand?'

I nod.

'So they had to get rid of us. One by one, they took our towns and villages. The military, the police, paramilitaries, they were all involved. They stole everything. They burned houses. They took people out and beat them, shot them. Women, children. It was terrible, Sanda. I began to lose all hope. I had never thought it would happen in my lifetime. Something like this.'

I lean in to hear because his voice has died to a whisper.

'We made it through that first year, I don't know how, but we did it. People helped each other – food, hiding places. Many Serbs helped us too, they didn't agree with what was happening. Then we heard there was a United Nations compound set up close by, in Srebrenica. We thought we could be safe there. But we couldn't get in.

'The town was attacked again and again – more lootings and killings. In the summer of '95, we left

Srebrenica for a town called Potočari, another United Nations safe zone. It was July and the heat was terrible. You and Senka cried all the time. We were so weak, so frightened. There was hardly any food or water, and many, many people died.

'Some of the soldiers were like animals. You cannot believe. They ... raped, they killed women and children. One time, I saw a soldier slit the throat of a baby in front of its mother. We were terrified. It was then that we were separated. I was left in the camp, and the women and children were put on a bus, I didn't know where to. We were told you were going to safety but we heard rumours that buses were being stopped and burned on the roadside, and the people killed. I thought I would never see you again.'

Here he breaks down and puts his hands across his face.

After a few minutes, he recovers and goes on: 'We, the men, knew we were going to be killed if we didn't act. We decided to make for the woods. To head to safety, to the government controlled area. We gathered what we could: scraps of food, a little water, only enough to last a couple of days, and we set out across country in the blazing heat. When the food was gone, we lived on leaves and slugs. We had no water left and we were exhausted. Only a few of us made it into our territory. We were starving, hallucinating, dressed in rags. I don't know how I survived; all I know is that it was the thought of you two and your mother that kept me alive. And then I was caught. I was put in a camp. That was bad enough, I nearly died. But to know that one of the people who put me there was my former student … She found me, and she told me what she'd done. I didn't see her again until … but she made sure I never forgot her. I was in there, and later in prison on some made-up charge, for five years.'

In the other room, I can hear Natalija and Peter, and the tick and knock of spoons on bowls.

He goes on, his voice rising and falling, 'When I got out of there, I knew I had to find you. I kept searching. I never gave up. I went everywhere. The Red Cross, the United Nations. I heard nothing. I followed every lead, however small. A friend found me a way out – to go to France. I'm a carpenter now – I make cabinets, tables, that sort of thing. From France too. I searched, I never gave up. I want you to know I never stopped looking.'

He starts to cry. I kneel down in front of him, and he takes me in his arms and presses me to him until I can barely breathe. He smells good: straw, wool, soap.

I gently break away: 'What about Senka?'

Branko attempts a smile and smudges the tears away with his sleeve.

'She doesn't know I'm here yet.' He takes my hands in his and together we stand up. 'Come on,' he says, 'Let's do it together.'

I open the door a crack and look into the kitchen. Peter's at the table with Senka and Andjela. They're both wrapped in blankets. Andjela is wolfing down soup and bread, and Senka holds a spoon dumbly in her hand. Her eyes open and close mechanically. There is a little run of soup on her chin. Peter's sitting next to Andjela, talking soothingly to her. It seems to be doing the trick. I see her smile shyly at him. Senka looks up at me as I come in, and lifts her arm to wipe the soup from her chin.

My twin sister.

When Senka sees Branko, she gasps. I go and sit down with her and cradle her frail form which goes from hot to cold, while he tells her how we were lost and found.

When he's finished, she says only one word: 'Majka?' *Mother.*

Branko swallows hard. He opens his mouth to speak, but before he can say anything, Andjela, who has been sitting quietly at the table all the while, stands up and goes quickly from the room.

I go out into the passageway and find her crouched against the wall, still with the blanket around her, her knees pulled into her chest. She raises her eyes to me. In them, I see real sadness and loneliness, and I know now what our joy at finding each other means for her. She gives a lopsided smile and makes the thumbs-up sign. I have to bite down hard on my lip not to cry.

'You'll be OK, Andjela,' I say. 'I'm going to look after you. You can stay with us.'

I lead her back into the kitchen. Branko and Senka are side by side, their heads touching. Peter and Natalija are standing by the door, hand in hand.

For the first time, it occurs to me to wonder what Branko's plan is. Is he intending to take us back with him? Is it presumptuous to ask if Andjela can come too?

And then I think again about how he probably has a new family. But I figure I've come so far, I have nothing to lose.

'Branko,' I say, 'could we ...'

He looks at me with his head on one side and a smile that somehow reminds me of Joe. I try again, 'Andjela ... I mean ... I don't know what's going to happen to her but ... could we ... Could we take her with us? To France?'

Before he can answer, Peter coughs awkwardly: 'Um. We ... it's just a thought ...'

He looks wildly at Natalija, who goes and kneels at Andjela's side and speaks to her softly. 'Andjela, Peter and I would like to offer you a home.'

Andjela's expression is a mix of joy and fear as she listens.

Natalija turns to face us. 'We've always wanted children but we couldn't have any. And it would make us so happy if we could give her a good life with us.'

Peter steps forward. 'You have your family now, Sanda. If Andjela will have us, we can be a family too.'

Andjela nods vigorously, smiling through her tears. Then everyone hugs everyone else, and Peter disappears and reappears moments later with a bottle of red wine. Branko reassures us that of course we're coming back with him, and he's going to get up early the next day and start making arrangements to get us papers to travel. This night is the best of my life so far. So much so, that I've almost forgotten about the letter from Joe.

Later, much later, after we're all fed and ever so slightly drunk, and Natalija and I have persuaded the girls to go to bed, she hands me the letter. It's a page folded in two with '*Sanda*' written on the blank side. My hands are shaking as I open it:

> *Dear Sanda*
> *I can't believe what's happened — that you were so close to getting what you wanted only to be betrayed. I can't bear the thought that someone might be hurting you. Three times I tried to get out to go look for you but they brought me back. Mum's made me go home with her. I hate her for it. I won't stop looking for you. Ever. You're amazing. I love you. J.*

I lean back in my chair and run my hands through my stubbly hair. He's in me, under my skin, and in my head where he's always been. Joe. My Joe.

I send him an email on Natalija's laptop. I know he's in hospital, I know he may not see it for a while but I do it anyway; all I say is: '*I'm back. I got your letter. I'll call soon. And, me too.*'

I go to bed with the letter under my pillow. Senka and I top and tail on the single bed in the room I slept in before. She moans and scratches at herself in her sleep and I can feel the unnatural heat off her body.

When I wake in the morning, Branko's already left on the early train to Belgrade to make arrangements for us to travel. Senka's feet are in a terrible state. I call Natalija to take a look. Her skin is paper thin with rosy blotches that she picks at constantly. Between us we give her a proper bath. She loves the hot bath water, and lies back and kicks her legs like a baby. I have to leave the room because I can't see through my tears any more. When I come back in, Natalija has lifted her out, wrapped her in a thick warm towel, and together we help her dry and get dressed. Natalija then goes to get cream for her feet and medicine for her fever. While we wait, Senka feels for my hand and squeezes it, and I know I'm home. When I'm with her, I'm home.

Later on, Senka's sitting up at the table eating bread and jam. She has jam on her elbows and butter on her chin. Clean and fed, she's just beginning to lose the hunted look in her eyes.

Natalija goes out after breakfast and leaves Peter to the business of searching out information on adoption. The inn stays closed for the day.

Natalija returns after a couple of hours, laden with bags. In them are clothes, medicines, bandages for Senka's feet and soft slippers while they heal, antiseptic cream for sores, antibiotics, lice powder and vitamin pills. We crowd round while she opens the other bags: for Andjela, there is a beautiful turquoise hoodie, a tartan mini-skirt and red tights with some black boots; for Senka, some jeans and the softest woollen striped jumper in green and blue. I get a little black mini-dress with a pair of blue tights. And for all of us: new underwear!

We're so excited, we disappear immediately to try on the clothes. Andjela is transfixed by the textures, the colours. She doesn't know what to do with tights so I help her on with them. Senka sits and watches us and clasps her hands. Andjela and I then help her into her new clothes, and she spends a long time turning around in front of the mirror.

I say, 'Senka – you're beautiful!'

Just over a week later, Branko gets a call from the authorities. They have documents for us to travel out of Serbia as soon as we've had blood tests to prove he's our father. Natalija says that she can get it done that afternoon. She has a colleague in the main hospital she can call.

Senka's terrified of the hospital, of the white coats and needles, but she follows our lead and lets the nurse take a little tube of blood; she looks as though she can barely spare any. I stay while they run other tests on her. As Natalija thought, she's malnourished and suffering from anaemia. Her skin and hair are very poor although Natalija's treatments are helping.

When we get the results, I think I feel properly hopeful for the first time ever. I suppose deep down I had my doubts. I guess when the rug is ripped from under you once, then maybe you're always ready for it to happen again. But now, after all we've been through, we have the answer we want: this man is our father. And we're going home. He's taking us home.

He's brought no pictures of home, but he talks about it. He lives in a village about thirty minutes from Bordeaux in an old house – at least two hundred years old. It's painted white, he says, with climbing roses and honeysuckle that cover the walls. There's a large garden at the back. He has his workshop in an outbuilding where he does his carpentry.

I'm scared but I have to ask, 'Do you have other children? Do you have a wife?'

He looks at me and strokes my cheek affectionately. 'You'll meet my family when you arrive. It will be good, I promise.'

From the window, I can see Peter and Natalija strolling across the square with Andjela. She's so changed. From the timid, racked creature I first met, she's turning into a confident, loving young woman. Her dark hair shines and her violet eyes are always smiling now. They already look like a family. Natalija's face is animated and happy as she listens to what Andjela is saying, and Peter's the proud father.

When they come in, I see he's holding a newspaper in his hand.

'Look, Sanda.'

23

On the front page of the newspaper is a picture of Kristina being taken into court: she's handcuffed between two grim-looking policemen. Her face is twisted into an indignant snarl. The sight of her crushes me, breaks me. I feel a toxic creep that works its way into me through every pore.

When Branko sees it, his mouth is set. 'I will make it up to you. You will be happy. You and Senka will be loved. I promise you. I promise. For always. My darling daughters, you have been treated so badly but we can heal this. We can make it better. I promise.'

I know I have my father and my sister now, and I shouldn't want more but my God I do. I want more. And the more that I want is Joe. It's all about Joe. It always has been.

Of course, going home means leaving home too. The inn has become a kind of home for us. I'll always remember it as the place I found my family, and where Andjela found hers.

Her adoption is going through. They tried but couldn't trace any family for her. Peter and Natalija have found a tutor who will help prepare her for school next year, and they're planning to teach her to read and write over the coming months. Peter's teaching her to play chess and she's getting really good at it. I love to watch him watching her, with his chin in his hands, as she considers her next move. They look after her with such tenderness. Natalija sits with her in the evenings, often with tears in her eyes. I think she's weeping for the childhood Andjela has lost and the love she could have given her. Saying goodbye to them after everything we've been through together is really hard.

I hug Peter and he lifts me up to face him. 'You look after your sister, girl.'

'I will!'

'It's going to be tough, Sanda – I mean, for her. You'll have to be –'

'I know! I know!'

'It's just there are going to be lots of surprises …'

'Surprises? What do you mean?'

'I … well, stuff's just going to be different. You know … stuff to take in…'

'Oh. Right. Yes, of course.'

Natalija comes up to me and wraps me in her arms, and I breathe in her lovely rosemary scent. She says simply, 'You will come back to visit I hope.'

I say, 'Of course. *Of course*. Thank you so much for all you've done. You've helped me to find my family.'

'And you've helped us to find ours.'

She smiles then and stands back so I can say good bye to Andjela. We look at each other and she touches my cheek very gently, just as she did that day in the dinner hall.

'Goodbye, Sanda,' she whispers in English.

'Goodbye. We'll see you soon.'

She turns to Senka and a look passes between them that tells at once of all the hardship and horror they have endured, and of all the hope that they have now.

I squeeze her hand and she steps back into the waiting arms of her new parents.

My sister, it turns out, is terrified of aeroplanes. And airports. And crowds. We find this out at the worst time, pushing through crowds at Belgrade airport to catch our plane. It's the floor that gets her at first. The way the strip lights are reflected on the marble, then the snapping of the display boards overhead. Branko and I walk close on either side of her.

The aeroplane is difficult too, and when we finally get her to her seat, she sits hunched over, hugging her knees, with her eyes shut tightly against the lights and noise. Branko and I glance at each other anxiously, and I see other passengers nudging each other and whispering. After a while, Senka falls asleep with her head hanging. I shift her so she's more comfortable, and the weight of her against me, the smell of her hair and the sound of her breathing makes me feel more than ever that, whatever happens next, I'm safe. Found.

We stop a few hours in Paris, then fly on to Bordeaux.

In Bordeaux, everything happens very quickly. Branko gets us a taxi back to his home town. His French is fluent, and I find myself wondering about getting by in the language if this is to be our home. Senka and I sit in the back, half-awake in the darkness, and I watch the headlights catch in her eyes. Branko talks to her, explaining where we are and how long the journey will take. She nods from time to time but I can see she's just overwhelmed.

And me? I don't know. I feel numb. I feel sick. I feel frightened but excited. I know because I'm rubbing and digging my thumbs into the palms of my hands. I'm so tired of waiting and hoping and wondering but I can't stop myself. I can't switch off that motor in my head. I want to sleep but I can't. It feels like I haven't slept for a million years. I know Branko's nervous too. Every so often, he drums his fingers on the dashboard and offers the driver some help on directions which it's clear are not needed. Deep in my pocket, folded into a square inch, is the letter from Joe.

After about half an hour, we come off the main road, carry on a few miles and then turn into a lane with high hedges on either side. In the distance, a little church spire thrusts up into the sky. The wind has picked up and with it the rain.

Branko turns to us and says, with a cracking voice, 'Here we are. You are home my children.'

24

In front of us, a barred gate, swinging open on its hinges, leads onto a gravel drive. The white house he's described to us stands in the middle of a large garden. It has high shuttered windows and climbing roses all over the front, just as he described it. There's an old bench by the front door and I wonder to myself if he made it. Pinned over the porch and around the windows is a trail of fairy lights. And at the door, shielding her eyes from our headlights, stands a slight figure: a woman.

She stays very still and as the car moves off and the beams sweep away, her face is in darkness, haloed by the fairy lights. Branko turns to us. I'm carrying my own and Senka's bags, and he motions to me to put them down. He smiles, puts his arms around us, and walks us to where the woman stands watching us.

She's small and slim, with her hair tied back in a bun, and she's wearing a soft jersey dress with pockets. She covers her mouth with both hands as we come into the hallway, and I see with a shock that one of her eyes is green, the other a violet blue. But the most striking thing about her, I only notice when she takes her hands from her face. All over her left cheek is a cluster of deep, pitted scars. Her mouth is buckled and misshapen on one side, and when she smiles, the scars curl and twist upwards.

Branko goes to her. He takes her arm through his and strokes her hand. They face us and he says quietly, 'Senka, Sanda, this is your mother.'

Senka cries out, puts her hand over her mouth and heaves forward onto the floor. At once, Branko is there to help her up. I find I can do nothing, say nothing. I look at the woman standing there, and she looks right back at me. And I see at once the person in the photograph that Branko sent out all over the world: a young woman in a polka dot dress shielding her eyes from the sun, with her two little girls by her side – my mother.

She speaks in English. 'I'm Elzina.'

'Elzina,' I repeat slowly, turning the name in my head. Branko speaks then, with an arm around Senka's shoulder as she rocks and watches our mother:

'We've had so many disappointments. So many times when we thought we'd found you but it turned out to be nothing. I wanted to be sure. I didn't tell your mother until I knew for sure. I didn't tell you because … because … well. I didn't know how to. I thought this would be better. That's why when you asked, I didn't give a straight answer. I hope you understand. I never thought this day would come. We are so, so happy to have you home with us.

Aren't we El?'

In answer, she comes to us and reaches out her arms. Tears are coursing down her scarred face. Shyly, I embrace her and there's the scent of roses. Cheek on cheek, I can feel her ravaged face, feel the tightening, the warp, as she smiles. And my tears fall on her shoulders and soak into the weave of her dress.

'Majka, Majka, Majka.' I now remember crying those words as I'm wrenched from her arms. The fuzzy picture I've carried in my head for so long is finally clear. It makes sense. I make sense. I've woken up.

Branko's crying too I see, but quietly to himself.

As we cling to our mother, I hear her say more to herself than anyone else: 'My children. My little ones.'

Later on, around the table in the kitchen, over home-made soup and bread, Elzina tells us her stories. Kristina was right. They did shoot her.

They were put on a bus with other women and children at Potočari. She was told they were going to safety. The bus drove up into the hills and, at a checkpoint on a lonely road, it was stopped. The Škorpioni were waiting. And with them, Kristina. The women and children were taken off the bus and made to stand in a field by the side of the road. They told them the bus had broken down, and they had to wait for a replacement.

They were all starving and exhausted. Our mother sat on the ground with Senka and me, apart from the others, and as she did so, Kristina spotted her. Elzina recognised her at once.

She tells us how Kristina was beautiful then: tall, poised but how her eyes were ice. 'She said, "You love these children, don't you? Look at you, how you hold them, how you care for them, how they cling to you. Don't look so frightened, I'm not going to kill them. But I'm going to take them. I'm going to watch them grow up without love, without hope. Without you." And the man with her, he took you both. I was screaming but she pushed me back. He put you in the jeep and came back, and the last thing I remember is him pointing his rifle at me.'

She heard later – she had no conscious memory – that, as panic took hold, the soldiers opened up their machine guns on the women and children. She was saved because other bodies fell on top of her. That night when all was quiet, she crawled out and limped away into the forest.

She was helped by an elderly couple who took pity on her. They took her in and nursed and hid her. She recovered a little, enough to escape to safety.

For years she searched for Branko, for us. She took work in a centre with children orphaned by the conflict, always hoping against hope that one day we would be brought in. And that was how, years later, she and Branko were reunited. Having finally got out of the camp and started looking for us in earnest, he went there one day following a lead.

They tried to make a new life but never stopped looking. Branko says their love for us and each other kept them strong.

That night in bed, the house sings me to sleep. It holds me. It's as though the house is a part of what I've been looking for all this time. A part of what's been missing, along with my family.

And in the morning, I wake to sweet-smelling linen and a jar of cornflowers on the dresser. The room looks out onto the lane that runs along the side of the house. There are hawthorn hedges and beech trees, their bare branches reaching into a silver sky.

I pad next door in my loose pyjamas, open the door to Senka's room and lean around the door. The gentle hum of her sleeping greets me. Her head is resting on her clasped hands. A low voice then from by the window: '*Sanda.*'

Our mother is there, sitting on a little chair. She smiles at me and beckons me in. I cross to her, kneel at her feet and put my head on her lap while her fingers weave in my hair.

'My heart is mending,' she says. 'To see you here to-gether, to see what I thought I would never see – it's closing a hole here.' And she places her hand on her chest.

I look up. 'What they did to you …'

She touches her scarred face. 'This is nothing. It means nothing. When it happened, in between, now. The real damage was always inside of me, and now you're here.'

The room spins into a snail shell, and she and I are curled in it for one, two minutes before she lifts my head, kisses me lightly, and presses something into my hand. It opens into my palm: an envelope with my name on it.

As I take it, she sits back and smiles, cupping her poor broken cheek. I look at her, puzzled, as I score my finger under the seal.

Untidy, slanting scrawl in heavy black pen. On lined file paper:

Look under the apple tree.

I look at my mother and there's that secret smile. She points to the window.

The window is old and it bulges out of the house. Under it, a seat has been built, covered with a thin cushion. I kneel up on this, put my hands on the window and look out. The garden stretches away down to a gate, and through it, I can see high rushes and a glint of water running through them. Beyond the stream is a field, where a number of fat, shrunken trees stand with twisted boughs. I go to ask her but she shakes her head and puts her finger to her lips.

Wet grass licks at my ankles as I make my way across to the little gate. The water is thick with weed that streams and trails like hair. I glance back for a moment at the house to see my mother at the upstairs window. She raises her hand in a shy wave and I wave back.

The stream is wide, and as I look about for something to steady myself to cross it, I see a figure, tall and dark, standing perfectly still a little way off through the trees. A breeze moves the branches around him.

'Joe!' I call. 'JOE!' I launch myself over the stream and run through the long grass to where he's waiting to catch me.

I'm against his chest then, breathing him into me. He draws me into him. He half pushes, half lifts me up against the tree and kisses me. His hands are on my back under my pyjama top, and I can feel the rough warmth of his palms on my shoulder blades as he pulls me against him.

He says, 'I was starting to think I'd never see you again.'

I look up at him and his eyes are full.

'Me too,' I say.

'I wish I'd stopped you going that day – or gone with you. Did they hurt you?'

'It's OK. It's OK now…'

'Christ,' he rakes a hand into his hair.

'Listen Joe …'

'I should have been there. I could have …'

I put my hand in his. 'It's OK. You're here now. How did you know where to find me?'

'I called Peter. I wanted to see you. Be here. When you …' but he's distracted.

I say, 'Listen. It doesn't matter. What happened. None of it. I've found my family, my real family, and I have you …' and then I think I shouldn't have said it because, *do* I have him? What do I mean by that? I mean he hasn't asked me to marry him. He's just …

'Stop it.'

'What?'

'I know what you're doing …'

'*What?* What am I doing?'

'You're worrying about what you've just said …'

'I … I …sorry. I just didn't want …'

He's laughing now. 'I know. I know. You didn't want to presume that you '*had*' me because maybe I just wanted to fly to Bordeaux which is nearly *five hundred miles* by the way, for a laugh, then I was just going to go home and forget about you?'

I nod slowly, but I'm smiling. 'And ...' he adds – I look up expectantly – 'STOP saying *sorry.*'

I push him against the tree, and he ends up with a quiff of lichen and cobwebs on his head. He pulls me towards him, and I feel his breath on me, warm and sweet.

He whispers, 'You remember what I told you once? In that van?'

'What?'

'How people notice you?'

'I ...well, I ...yes.'

Of course I remember. I remember every conversation we've ever had; even back at school in Year Ten when he once asked me the way to Room 104. Tragic. Totally tragic.

'Well. I meant it. You are beautiful. You're ... you're lovely.'

I don't know what to say because '*No, I'm not ...*' would just be so completely lame and wrong right now. I'm thinking what to say when there's a call from the house.

My mother: 'Come and have some breakfast you two!'

Before we go, he leans in and kisses me hard on the lips, his mouth is open and his lips are firm and he tastes so good. And for a full minute after, when my head is spinning, he takes my face in his hands, and looks and looks and looks at me. Into me. Inside of me. And he fills me up with him.

And arm in arm, we track back through the grass and the fallen apples to where my family are waiting.

25

As the months pass, we're really starting to feel like a family.

It's been a difficult ride for Senka, it's been hard for her to be in a family, but she and I are very close. Her reading and writing are going well, but her real love is drawing. She draws everything she sees: sparkling rivers over stones, the paint-box brightness of meadow flowers in the high grasses. She's drawn hundreds of pictures of our mother and father in her own scratchy style.

They've bought her a set of pens and inks in different colours, which she loves. Possessions are still so new to her that she guards them very closely. She's learning French and English now, and while she's not yet ready for school, she has a tutor. She's really close to Branko, and finds being away from him hard. She helps him in his wood shop and is popular with the customers. She perches on the chair in his office, leaning on one elbow, drawing.

As for me, the transition has been easier. My French

is getting better, I go to a local school and I'm doing my Baccalaureate. School is OK now. I miss Lauren but we talk all the time. She tells me she's impressed: I guess maybe I found my inner cool. I can be by myself or with other people and it doesn't bother me. I don't get tongue-tied or nervous any more. What happened to me has changed me forever. One thing's for sure, I don't take any shit from anyone. Ever.

I'm doing a lot of writing. I've bought a journal and I'm recording my parents' stories. I've spent long evenings with my mother, listening to her and transcribing her words. I'm involved with a charity now that works with orphanages in Eastern Europe, and I'm planning to spend part of this summer helping on a building project in Romania.

I email Andjela most weeks, and she's doing really well. She goes to the local school and has made some friends. Peter has bought her a bulldog puppy and she goes walking in the pine woods with him. If I close my eyes, I can still feel the ferns brushing my legs and smell the zest of pine on the air. Last time she wrote, she sent me a photo. She's standing in front of the inn in the little square, arm in arm with Natalija. They are squinting in the sun, and smiling. Her hair is cut into a smart bob, and she looks well fed and happy.

They're coming over at Christmas and I'm starting to think of a cool present for her. Natalija says she's mad on clothes, so when I go to the city, I'll look for something she might like.

I haven't been back to the street in London. I know

some day I must, but right now I can't bring myself to. It holds so many bad memories and I don't want to think of them now. I hear about Kristina from time to time on the news. She's on remand awaiting trial for war crimes in the International Criminal Court. She could be put away for a long time. I tried to make contact through her solicitor once but was told she had no wish to be in touch. I guess that was always the way it was going to be. I think maybe that was the hardest thing about coming here: remembering my life before. What I had and what I didn't have and the way I used to feel.

Joe and I see each other as much as we can. We're going travelling after school ends. He comes to me or I go to London. He's just passed his driving test, and last weekend, he drove over in his mum's car and took me out to Arcachon by the sea. We sat on the dunes under a blanket and ate chips. He threw one into the air and a seagull dipped and caught it mid-flight. And I told him how much I loved him. I do.

ACKNOWLEDGMENTS

'Thank you' is a rather silly expression. It's what we say when we're handed a plate of peas or when someone opens the door for us.

I'd like to take some of those thin little 'thank you's and knit them into an enormous, hairy patchwork quilt of 'thank you's. And in every patch, there'd be a name: of friends who read bits, encouraged me, were unfailingly positive, offered suggestions, and listened to me whining about rejections and semi-colons.

Thank you to my wonderful editor Sara, who saw it a long time ago, and made me have faith in it as something that might perhaps work – I've learned so much from you, babe.

Thank you to Catherine, for your encouraging words and for the final top and tail.

Thank you to my dear stepsons: Jack, James and Oliver, who always say, 'How's the book going?' and 'Like the cover, Jane'.

Thank you to my excellent friend and partner in crime at Blowfish, Lisa, whose brilliant brain drilled down into every corner of this book, tweezing out mad inconsistencies and horrible grammatical errors.

Thank you to my husband, TB, who's been rowing our little boat against the tide and without whom I wouldn't have written a single word. Ever.

Thank you to my three children, who've watched me cry and squirm and agonise over plot and character and who've given me countless ideas and space and snuggles and practical help and wonderful, bountiful, encouragement and love.

Thank you.

The idea for *The Edge of Me* came to me a long time ago. The Bosnian War was happening when my own children were little and because I was interested in writing a story with its roots in war, I chose this one.

Many children on all sides were orphaned or separated from their loved ones. Some were taken like Sanda; many grew up scarred and troubled.

A book I loved as a child was *The Silver Sword* by Ian Serraillier. It's set in war-torn Europe in the Second World War about three children whose parents are taken away and who undertake a perilous and frightening journey out of Nazi occupied Poland and on into safety in Switzerland. It's a book about courage when everything is lost and everyone is displaced. It's also about salvation.

In *The Edge of Me*, Sanda finds the courage to fight for what's right when everything is wrong and twisted; she also finds herself and what was missing all along.

NOTE:

The *Scorpions* were a Bosnian Serb paramilitary organisation that was very active in the Bosnian War and responsible for many atrocities. That they are still operating to this day, as suggested in the book, is, to my knowledge, entirely fictitious.

To read more about the Bosnian conflict, please visit the Blowfish Books website: www.blowfishbooks.com

If you have enjoyed this book, please do leave a nice review on our Amazon page.

Coming soon from Jane Brittan:

BAD BLOOD

The first instalment of Jane Brittan's edgy, fast-paced thriller series follows Ben and Sophy as Ben struggles to make sense of what happened to his father, what he left behind when he died and why certain people seem so interested in it.

The stakes are high from the very start and the more he finds out, the worse they get.

His father was a scientist. It's only later that Ben finds out exactly what kind of scientist. And that's when things get dangerous …